Drowning in Christmas

by

Judith K. Ivie

Mainly Murder Press, LLC

PO Box 290586
Wethersfield, CT 06109-0586
www.mainlymurderpress.com

Mainly Murder Press

Copy Editor: Jennafer Sprankle
Executive Editor: Judith K. Ivie
Cover Designer: Patricia L. Foltz

All rights reserved

Copyright © 2010 by Judith K. Ivie
ISBN 978-0-9827952-5-5

Published in the United States of America
2010
Mainly Murder Press
PO Box 290586
Wethersfield, CT 06109-0586
www.MainlyMurderPress.com

Dedicated with appreciation and affection to

Dr. Linda Dupont, Cindy, Beth, Jana,
Natalie, Mary Jean, T.J., Jude, Dr. Braun,
and all of the other caring staff members of
Catzablanca Cat Clinic & Hospital
in Rocky Hill, Connecticut,
who have contributed immeasurably
over the years to the health and well-being of
the feline members of our family
… and the peace of mind of their owners

Praise for the Kate Lawrence Mysteries

[*Drowning in Christmas*] would be fun to read any time of the year. ... Kate Lawrence is a heroine who's easy to like. And if you're familiar with central Connecticut, that's just an added bonus!

Carole Shmurak, author, The Susan Lombardi Mysteries

Waiting for Armando is a wonderful mix of characters ... a real slice of life.

Lighthouse Literary Reviews

Ms. Ivie's kicky turn of phrase made *Murder on Old Main Street* a fun read.

Mystery Lovers Corner

More than an investigation of the crime, *A Skeleton in the Closet* is also an exploration of human interaction.

John Valeri, examiner.com

A Skeleton in the Closet is a delightful cozy mystery New England style ... a densely packed little read that is both light and entertaining.

The Midwest Book Review

One of the things I love about Ivie's characters is that they are not twenty-something Nancy Drews. They are mature, grown-up women with full lives and vivid pasts.

Marlene Pyle, The Genreview.com

Introduction

I was born and raised in central Connecticut, and I raised my own children here. We have always considered ourselves fortunate to have the Wadsworth Atheneum Museum of Art, America's oldest public art museum, right here in Hartford and to be able to enjoy its amazing collection of American and European art during innumerable visits over the years.

For as long as we can remember, the Wadsworth's Festival of Trees & Traditions has anchored our holiday season, as I know it has for thousands of others. Beautifully orchestrated by the Women's Committee of the Atheneum, the Festival showcases the best of our Connecticut community. Hundreds of breathtaking holiday creations crafted by local artists, school children, and volunteers are enhanced by the musical offerings of local choirs and musicians. Together, these talented community members transform the first floor of the Museum into a magical holiday wonderland. It's really something to experience.

What better setting for a Christmas murder mystery?

That's what I thought, too. Enjoy.

Judith K. Ivie

 **One**

"I wouldn't ask you," said my ex-husband, "but I'm desperate. I really need your help here."

"No," I said.

"Did you hear the desperate part, Kate?" Michael wisely refrained from whining, which he knew would only make me crankier. Instead, he allowed sufficient time to pass for his surprising request to replay in my mind. Yes, the man had to be on the edge.

I sighed heavily and closed my partner Strutter's copy of *A Homemade Holiday*, which was supposed to be giving me great ideas on how to cook a Christmas goose. Something told me that my goose was pretty well cooked already. As ex-husbands go, mine was about as agreeable as they get, but this conversation sounded like big trouble to me. I closed my eyes and tried to ignore the headache that began to throb through my temples.

"You know I don't even attend weddings anymore, Michael, let alone organize one. Not now, not ever again. I endured enough family weddings, birthdays, anniversary parties, and holiday gatherings in the twenty-two years we were married to last me the rest of my life. I just send a lovely gift and decline the invitation. I'm done, through, finished. Am I getting through to you?"

"The fact that I'm even asking you should give you some idea of my state of mind." Michael dropped his voice several decibels, the better to keep our conversation private from his present wife, I presumed. "Sheila already has her hands full with her teaching and the holiday pageant at the school, plus her mother will be spending Christmas with us this year." He paused to let the full horror of having Sheila's ditzy maternal relative as a houseguest sink in. "Having a wedding in this little apartment would be impossible under the best of circumstances, but right now ..." He trailed off miserably.

Grudgingly, I admitted that he had a point. After years of working and saving, he and Sheila were finally on the verge of seeing their dream house, currently under construction on Lake Pocotopaug, become a reality. Having been lucky enough to sell their previous house sooner than expected in the current crummy real estate market, they were waiting out the final months of construction in a one-bedroom rental, not the ideal setting for a family wedding.

"So rent the church hall or the V.F.W. or a room at the community center," I countered weakly, knowing that would never do. Schmidts were married at home. It was a family tradition with which I was well acquainted. Michael and I had been married in his parents' living room nearly thirty years ago, and we had hosted our share of nuptials for cousins and nieces in our own home in the ensuing years. Still, I wasn't caving in without a fight this time. I had quite enough on my plate already.

Michael regrouped and tried another approach. "We just need your house for the afternoon. Well, maybe the evening, too. There has to be a little party after the ceremony. You and Armando wouldn't even have to be there, if you didn't want to be. The caterer will do absolutely everything, including the clean-up. It's just family and a few friends." He played his ace. "Come on, Kate. I wouldn't ask you, but you are Jeff's godmother, after all. If you won't do it for me, do it for him."

That one hit the mark. When it comes to family ties, I'm notoriously unsentimental. I firmly believe that you can choose your friends, but your relatives are thrust upon you without your having any say in the matter. I have no great fondness for my mother's and father's numerous kinfolk, so I have aunties and first cousins I literally wouldn't recognize on the street; but for Michael's nephew Jeff, I have a soft spot. He's the youngest of the three sons of Michael's late brother and his wife, who were taken in an automobile accident several years ago.

Jeff's quirky outlook and lightning-quick wit endear him to me, as well as to my son Joey and daughter Emma, above all of their less-interesting cousins. Besides, as Michael pointed out, I am Jeff's godmother, however reluctantly I had agreed to assume that role upon his birth. I had performed my duties casually in the twenty-five years since, but now that Jeff's parents were no longer among us, who else was there to help him out with his wedding? My heart softened.

I carried the phone and my coffee mug to the back windows of my freestanding condominium unit and gazed at the gray December landscape. My elderly cat Jasmine was perched on the back of the sofa. She stared fixedly at three wild turkeys pecking contentedly on the snowless lawn. No doubt they were grateful to have dodged a bullet now that Thanksgiving was safely past.

"When is this wedding in my house that I don't have to attend supposed to take place?"

Sensing that he still had a shot, Michael brightened. "The twenty-seventh, which is the Sunday after Christmas. Jeff has to leave for North Carolina two days later, which is why he and Donna decided to move up their wedding date. The University offers housing for married graduate students only. Hey, you won't even have to decorate, since even you must leave your Christmas stuff up until New Year's Day."

I ignored this slur on my holiday spirit. "Great. You do realize that Emma is bringing her new boyfriend here on Christmas Eve to meet us. Jared, I think this one is named, and I'm expected to do the whole Norman Rockwell bit. Chestnuts roasting, pumpkin pie, et cetera et cetera. She's gone a little nuts over this guy, and she's taking me with her. When you called, I was looking at recipes for roast goose."

"You're cooking a goose?" The disbelief in Michael's voice was evident. Then, straying from the point as he often did, "Why not turkey?"

I considered my feathered friends, now making their leisurely way toward the marsh that bordered The Birches. They strolled the grounds of our Wethersfield, Connecticut condominium community daily and roosted in the surrounding trees at night. Before I'd come to live here, I hadn't known that turkeys can fly. Now I regularly watched them helicopter up to their favorite branches as the sun slipped beneath the horizon.

"Too much like pets, I guess." Truth be told, I wasn't much looking forward to roasting a goose either. The things we do for our children. "So the situation is that I'm entertaining Emma's steady on Thursday evening, and three days later, I'm throwing a wedding." I sighed again. Well, in for a penny, in for a pound, and it was for Jeff and his absolutely darling fiancée Donna, whom he had been dating since high school.

I could almost hear the grin of relief breaking across Michael's amiable face. "I'm telling you, this caterer is incredible. You won't have to lift a finger, Kate. He and his staff will do everything ... food, flowers, music, photographer. They bring everything in and take everything away afterwards. Sheila's friend Millie used him for her daughter's wedding last summer."

The headache teased behind my eyes again, and I interrupted Michael's rhapsodic litany. "Okay, okay, I get it. I won't have to do a thing." *Yeah, right.* "So send out the invitations, and let's get it done," I said rashly. "Now can I go to work, please?"

"You bet, sure! Thanks a million, Katie. You're the best. We'll talk again in a couple of days." He was gone before I could take back my words. *Not that I would,* I amended my thoughts guiltily. I swallowed the last of my tepid coffee and watched the turkeys melt into the marsh, becoming one with the colors of the dried undergrowth. Now you see them, now you don't. *Invisibility has its appeal,* I thought wistfully. At the moment, I was feeling far too visible, not to mention vulnerable, on several fronts.

Work was one of them. For the past two years, since meeting at the downtown Hartford law firm where we all worked at that time, my friends and partners Margo Harkness, nee Farnsworth, and Charlene "Strutter" Putnam, nee Tuttle, had owned and operated MACK Realty in Wethersfield's historic district. Starting our own business had been an adventure, to say the least, and the hot real estate market had taken us on a wild ride.

A couple of months ago, the financial market had crashed, taking real estate and every other kind of sales down with it. Temporarily, at least, MACK Realty operated out of Margo's dining room, where she and Strutter had hunkered down to weather the storm. Our receptionist Jenny had opted to return to UConn Law School full time. Because I had administrative and computer skills, I decided to put them to good use in a temporary position in the local office of Unified Christian Charities, situated in Hartford.

"We need you!" had been Sister Marguerite's opening salvo. Sister Marguerite is the CEO of Unified Christian Charities, and she is one smart cookie. Notwithstanding the fact that I haven't seen the inside of a church in more than a decade, she and I have worked together on several charitable endeavors over the years and become firm friends in the process. She is unlike any other nun I have ever met, not that I've met many. In fact, her lack of sanctimony and earthy sense of humor have seen me through more than a few dreary fundraising dinners.

Almost before the moving van carrying MACK Realty's office furniture to a storage facility had disappeared over the horizon, the wily sister had left a message on my answering machine, shoring up my wounded ego with a job offer. "Mary Alice is expecting her fourth baby, saints preserve us, and this time, her doctor insists that she take to her bed for the last two weeks, although how a woman who already has three little ones manages that is beyond me. So here I am, a rudderless ship sinking fast in a sea of meetings and paperwork, plus the holiday fundraiser at the Wadsworth that's hard upon us. Can you help me out, Katie? It's not forever, just for a couple of weeks until the child is born and Mary Alice's mum arrives to take charge of the household," she wheedled.

I knew I was being manipulated, which was always a good bet when dealing with Sister, but her offer did seem to be the answer to a prayer, no pun intended. Without MACK Realty taking up sixty hours a week of my time, I was feeling more than a little rudderless myself. My housemate and longtime love, Armando Velasquez, had just departed to San Diego on an assignment for his employer, TeleCom International. So what with one thing and another, time stretched emptily ahead of me. A temporary assignment would be just the thing to fill the gap, and a little money coming in wouldn't hurt. What better way to use my time than helping out my old friend Sister Marguerite?

Today was to be my first day on the job, and I hurried to get myself together. Without the wild turkeys to offer entertainment, Jasmine trailed after me down the hall to my bedroom. She was missing Simon, her feline companion of more than fifteen years. He had recently succumbed to a combination of health issues rooted in old age, devastating our household. I knew Jasmine was lonely, but Simon had been my devoted old boy, my best buddy. I still grieved for him and couldn't face bringing a newcomer into the house. *Not yet, but as soon as I can,* I promised Jasmine silently. As I rushed about from bedroom to bathroom to closet, she settled herself on the foot of my bed, where she knew the mid-morning sun would fall, and was soon snoozing. This afternoon, she would return to the living room, where the west-facing windows would make the most of the wintry sunshine on the sofa.

After a fast shower and five minutes in front of the mirror with my blow dryer and minimal make-up, I hurried into a navy blue pantsuit and tucked a gauzy scarf with a wild floral print into the neckline. I jammed my feet into low-heeled pumps and blew Jasmine a kiss on my way to the front-hall coat closet, not that she noticed. Two minutes later, I was backing my Jetta out of the garage.

All things considered, I was feeling pretty chipper. Armando might be gone for a week or so, but I had never minded solitude. Part of me was looking forward to having some of it for a while. Still, it was good to have somewhere to go and useful work to do. Now that I was once again gainfully employed, however temporarily, I would be alone only in the evenings, and there was always the telephone. Armando has a wonderful telephone voice, a warm baritone touched with a Spanish accent. In the early days of our relationship, some six years ago, I had looked forward eagerly to his evening calls. Now that I knew all of the other sexy qualities that went along with the voice, I found myself smiling in anticipation once again.

The drive into Hartford on I-91 wasn't quite as frightening as I had remembered. Perhaps the truly suicidal commuters got on the road earlier in the morning. For whatever reason, I was allowed to lollygag along at a mere ten miles per hour over the posted speed limit without being harassed, which gave me an opportunity to absorb the changed city skyline. The Travelers tower, which along with the Old State House had been Hartford's most identifiable structure during my growing-up years, had been encircled by newer, taller structures. These included the Phoenix Insurance building, an oddly boat-like structure; the Gold Building, which housed United Technologies and more than twenty additional floors of corporate offices; two buildings of pink stone that overlooked the Connecticut River; and the newest additions to the city scene, a modern convention center and adjoining Marriott Hotel. Several blocks removed from this cluster, but still tall enough to be seen from the highway, were CityPlace, whose slanted green roof resembled a beret, and the CIGNA building at the corner of Church and Trumbull Streets. Standing cheek-by-jowl with the old brownstones and more conventional downtown structures, the new additions had transformed a fairly humdrum skyline into one that invited admiration.

I eased off the highway onto the sharply curved ramp that led beneath an overpass bearing the image of the Charter Oak, then swooped into Pulaski Circle with the rest of the traffic. As Sister Marguerite had instructed, I swung around the circle to Elm Street, which ran between Bushnell Park and the block anchored by the Bushnell Memorial Theater. It was a place that held magical memories for me and most other Connecticut theater-goers, as well as visitors who came by the busload. Armando and I had shared many wonderful evenings there together.

Pausing at the light, I gazed straight ahead at the gleaming dome of the State Capitol. The Legislature must be in session, I surmised from the packed parking lot and plethora of Capitol Police in the area. No doubt the lawmakers were in a last-minute flurry, trying to get pending legislation passed before the lawmakers could adjourn for the holidays.

The light changed, and I swung left past the Capitol building and right onto Capitol Avenue, which I followed several blocks past the State Library, Legislative Office Building, and assorted residential and commercial structures. A right onto Flower Street took me up the grade leading to Farmington Avenue and the area of Hartford referred to by the locals as Asylum Hill. It had been so nicknamed for the Asylum for the Education and Instruction of Deaf and Dumb Persons that had commanded the hill until around 1920. Then the institution was moved to West Hartford and more appropriately renamed the American School for the Deaf.

Today, the king of the hill was The Hartford Insurance Group. *No, it was now The Hartford Financial Services Group,* I reminded myself. It was one of the many huge insurers, including The Travelers and Aetna, that had given Hartford its national identity as the Insurance City.

Another lengthy traffic light gave me a chance to check out the current landscape of the Hill. I had never really paid much attention before, but now I took note of the churches that competed for pride of place. Among the older edifices were Emanuel Lutheran, which I had already passed on Capitol Avenue, Asylum Hill Congregational, and Trinity Episcopal, but there could be no question that The Cathedral of St. Joseph dominated the area.

When the light finally changed, I headed west toward

the small building in the shadow of the Cathedral, which housed the administrative staff of United Christian Charities. The organization was entirely ecumenical, Sister Marguerite had hastened to assure me, and served people in need throughout the region without regard to religious affiliation "or not," she had twinkled at me, well aware of my lack of religious convictions. "We welcome even the heathens among us, Katie, so fear not." Although she had spoken in jest, I wondered if that was how she secretly thought of me.

I parked and locked the Jetta up tight, mindful of Sister Marguerite's warning that this was no longer the safest of neighborhoods, and made my way to the back entrance of the humble building that had once been a two-family house. I pressed the electronic doorbell and faced the monitor, trying to look as unthreatening as possible. "Can I help you?" a woman greeted me in a British accent that not even this system could distort completely.

"Kate Lawrence here to see Sister Marguerite," I offered obediently. "She's expecting me." I was promptly buzzed through the outer door and climbed a half-staircase to the interior door, where I paused, suddenly weary. Here I was, facing yet another new job in a new location, my third such transition in as many years. *It could be worse,* I told myself firmly. *I could have nowhere to go and nothing to do. Sister Marguerite needs my help, and at this particular moment, that feels pretty darned good.* I took a deep breath, plastered a smile on my face, and turned the doorknob. Nothing happened. Then more buzzing led me to understand that this door, too, was locked electronically and had been similarly released by the receptionist.

"Goodness," I joked, approaching her desk. "I must be pretty shifty looking to require all these security precautions. I'm Kate Lawrence. I believe Sister Marguerite is expecting me this morning."

"It's not you," the pleasant-faced brunette apologized. "It's become an unfortunate fact of life that we have to keep both doors locked at all times, whether we're in the building or not. Too many bad experiences, I'm afraid."

"Wow, do you mean you've actually been robbed?"

She shrugged. "A couple of break-ins. Nothing at gunpoint or anything. I'm Shirley, by the way. Please hang your coat over there on the rack. Coffee's fresh. I'll tell Sister you're here." She waved in the general direction of a coat rack and a tiny kitchenette behind it where a coffee urn and mugs stood waiting on the counter. I hung my parka on a hanger and decided against more coffee. Instead, I admired Shirley's impressive array of potted plants, which thrived in the sunshine streaming through a window beside her desk.

Although small and somewhat cramped, the reception area had a friendly feel to it. The murmur of Monday-morning conversations among congenial coworkers met my ears, a poignant reminder of other Monday mornings at MACK Realty. I quickly turned the page on that thought and perched on one of the three chairs which, along with a small corner table, constituted the anteroom's entire furnishings. I struggled to get myself into a serene frame of mind, suitable for interaction with these kindly, gentle people who were about to become my temporary colleagues.

"Jesus, Mary and Joseph!"

My mouth dropped open, but Shirley didn't turn a hair at this surprising outburst from some interior office. Sister Marguerite appeared from behind a door at the end of a short hallway. She shoved it open energetically and hustled out to greet me. "What kind of a knucklehead takes up busy people's time on a Monday morning trying to sell them things over the phone, I ask you?"

Shirley calmly continued festooning a rather dusty plastic fir tree that occupied the tabletop next to my chair.

"Sorry, m'dear," Sister Marguerite apologized to me. "Telemarketers have driven more pious women than I to bad language and strong drink. Shirley, how many of these trees have you got in this place, for the love of God? I feel as if I'm suffocating in tinsel." A twinkle in her eye softened her words. Shirley merely grinned and went on decorating the already overburdened tree.

"Come in, come in," Sister Marguerite urged me and reversed direction. I scrambled after her down the short hallway, which was crowded with filing cabinets and overflowing bookshelves. Sister bustled into her office and addressed her guest chair. "Off with you now." She made shooing motions, and a fat poodle, which I had mistaken for an overstuffed pillow, lumbered to the floor. "Go to your bed, Aloysius." The dog wagged his stub of a tail to show there were no hard feelings and made his way arthritically to a snug pet bed behind his mistress's desk. "I shouldn't allow him on the furniture, I know, but he's quite an old fellow now," Sister explained. "Sit, sit!"

I sat. My eyes welled with grief for my own old pet, and I blinked the tears away. Two lines rang simultaneously on Sister Marguerite's phone, which she ignored. A tiny woman with gray hair stuck her head in the door. "Is this a good time to get some things signed, Sister? Oh, sorry," she amended, spotting me. "I didn't see you sitting there. Another time." And she was gone.

An hour later, I sat in a cramped conference room with the organizers of the annual UCC holiday fundraising event, a cocktail party and auction scheduled for this very Thursday evening. I had been introduced as Mary Alice's temporary replacement, warmly welcomed, and promptly buried in an avalanche of logistical details concerning the annual gala to be held at one of the crown jewels of Hartford's cultural community, the Wadsworth Atheneum Museum of Art.

The castle-like building was the oldest public art museum in the United States and the largest one in Connecticut. The Museum was particularly beautiful at this time of year. Thousands of additional visitors were attracted to its annual Festival of Trees & Traditions, a huge display of Christmas trees, wreaths, and other decorations constructed by local organizations and individuals and donated to be sold for the benefit of the Museum. That made the UCC gathering a fundraiser-within-a-fundraiser, so to speak.

The petite woman who had stopped by Sister Marguerite's office earlier turned out to be Lois Billard, the committee chair. She gave brisk updates on the budget, catering, entertainment, raffle contributions, and RSVPs received to date, which I struggled to take in. My head was spinning. It was clear that this was a major social occasion of the Hartford social season, and despite the downturn in the economy, this year's turnout was going to be a record setter. As Lois outlined the schedule for the evening, it was apparent that the major players from every segment of the business community would be present, as well as leading clergy from all of the Catholic, Protestant and Jewish denominations in the region.

The plan was to gather everyone in a prominent location, dazzle them with ambience, mellow them out with heavy hors d'oeuvres and spectacular wines donated by some of Connecticut's finest eateries and vineyards, then begin the auction. "Liquor them up and get those wallets open," was Lois's candid plan of action. "Then, just when they may be feeling they've overspent a tad, we'll bring in Santa Claus to distribute the goodie bags filled with gift certificates and enough electronic toys to thaw the tightest wad among them." She grinned at the assembled committee members, who chuckled appreciatively. Obviously, these people were not nearly as strait-laced as I had imagined them to be.

I had to admit that I quite looked forward to Thursday evening. "Who plays Santa?" I couldn't help asking. Sister Marguerite was quick to reply.

"Why, our very own Santa, of course," she smiled, gesturing to the bespectacled, middle-aged gentleman beside her who had sat quietly throughout the meeting and resembled Kris Kringle not at all. "Meet James O'Halloran, our chief financial officer, Kate. He's been playing Santa for us for nearly thirty years now. Says it makes a nice change from counting our beans the rest of the time."

"After all these years, I'm beginning to look the part," O'Halloran joked along, patting his flat belly as if it were round. "I believe I know one of your business partners, Ms. Lawrence. My wife and I bought a house in Wethersfield a couple of years back, and she had the listing. Cheryl? Sharmaine? Anyway, a delightful lady. Made the experience relatively painless, as I recall."

"Charlene Putnam," I smiled, "and yes, she is."

"James' wife Mary is a mainstay of the Wadsworth Atheneum's Women's Committee, which was how we managed to book that amazing space for our most important fundraiser of the year—and during the Festival of Trees, no less," Sister Marguerite beamed. "Of course, it took even Mary two years to pull it off," she added wryly, and everyone chuckled.

On that note, the meeting adjourned, and the staff quickly scattered to pursue their various last-minute assignments. Mine was to keep track of all of the other assignments and serve as the focal point for all gala-related communications in addition to answering Sister Marguerite's phone, screening incoming requests, and assisting with the daily business of the UCC, which was helping local people in need to cope with their current crises.

With Connecticut's unemployment rate threatening to become the highest in history, the stream of requests for help continued unabated throughout the afternoon, which whirled by in a blur. Just before five o'clock, the steeple bell of Asylum Hill Congregational Church rang out. "Two minute warning!" Sister Marguerite called out cheerily, and the staff members scurrying in and out of each other's offices and cubicles heaved a collective sigh of relief. "Quitting time, don't you know," Sister explained, "but that bell is a little off."

"Does it ring all day?" I asked in amazement. Until this moment, I had been unaware of it.

"Every hour on the hour," she assured me, "and two minutes early for every blessed one of them. Well, that's it for me, Katie girl. Come along, Aloysius, you spoiled dog. Time for us to get our supper and see if we can still manage a little walk between us." The poodle, who had been waiting patiently by Sister's briefcase, thumped his stubby tail on the carpet and creaked to his feet. She snapped a leash on his collar and picked up the briefcase, which bulged with paperwork to be attended to after dinner, no doubt. "Thanks for everything, m'dear," she said, patting my shoulder in passing as they headed for the door. "Can we expect you back tomorrow?"

"I'll be back," I assured her.

I let myself out into the parking lot, making sure that the door locked firmly behind me, as I had been instructed to do. The early darkness never failed to surprise me on these December evenings, but the lot was well lit. I joined the other going-homers in the late afternoon traffic and crept from traffic light to traffic light, reflecting on the events of the day.

Now that I had the time to notice, I realized how weary I was. A few days ago, I had been sitting in my recliner planning my next career move. Now I was orchestrating a Martha Stewart Christmas Eve for Emma's new beau, hosting my nephew's holiday wedding, and juggling the myriad details of the UCC's gala fundraiser. It wasn't surprising that I felt as if I were drowning in Christmas.

What I didn't know was that I was about to go under for the third time.

Two

"I can't believe Jeff is getting married." Emma, on the phone with me before work on Wednesday morning, was obviously jolted by the news. "He's younger than I am."

"What's that got to do with anything?" I wanted to know. "Is it a competition?"

She was reassuringly scornful. "I could have gotten married about six times since I turned fifteen, as you well know. It's not his age. I'm just astounded that he's getting married at all. He's such a maverick, and he and Donna have been doing just fine the way they are, like you and Armando, you know?"

I swallowed guiltily. Despite my determination never to marry again, about which I had been vociferous, Armando and I had had several conversations over the past year on the subject of marriage, specifically, the possibility of ours. *Never say never.* "Well, we can't know what prompts these things. Maybe Donna needs health insurance, and Jeff's employer won't provide coverage for domestic partners. Circumstances back people into corners sometimes."

She considered that possibility. "I suppose. Do you think that might ever happen to you and Armando?"

"The way this real estate market is shaping up, I wouldn't discount the idea altogether," I hedged. "People have gotten married for worse reasons, and if they're committed to each other anyway, why not?" I cleared my throat. "Of course, plenty of people still seem to want to get married for more romantic reasons, you know, stand up in front of their friends and families, say the words, take the vow."

Emma digested this surprising commentary from me in silence but forbore to grill me further on the subject. "Whatever. So Jeff's getting married, and Daddy has volunteered you to host the big event. Is that about the size of it?"

I hastened to soften her father's part in this scenario. "Pretty much, but you know he would have had it at his place if he could have. It's just not possible. Plus, there's a terrific caterer who's agreed to do most of the work."

Emma laughed. "Yeah, right. He'll sail in forty-five minutes before the ceremony, unload a bunch of food, and go outside to have a cigarette. What about the table set-ups and the drinks and the decorations? How about flowers, photographs? Who's sending out the invitations and tracking the responses? Are Jeff and Donna registered someplace so people will have a clue about gifts?" She paused for breath.

"Good grief, are all of those things up to me to arrange?"

She chuckled mirthlessly. "You know that movie where Katherine Heigl has been a bridesmaid a couple of dozen times? Well, I'm thirty, and I have a lot of girlfriends. Take my word for it. There's a ton of work involved here. The good news is, a lot of the arrangements should be taken care of by the maid or matron of honor. Who's that going to be?"

My knowledge of the details of this wedding was sketchy, at best. "I don't know. Are you volunteering?"

"Heck, no, I'm not volunteering. I just need to know who to call to get this show on the road."

My heart lifted as I sensed help on the horizon. "You're willing to do that?"

I could hear the smile in her voice. "That's why you called me, isn't it? Since I already have you doing the traditional New England Christmas Eve bit on my behalf, the least I can do is help you out with this wedding. A wedding!" I heard her slap her forehead. "This is going to be some kind of Christmas, isn't it?" Was I imagining it, or was Emma actually enjoying this?

"Some kind," I agreed cautiously. I had always found the holidays somewhat overwhelming, and until this year, I thought Emma felt the same way. Maybe she harbored some Norman Rockwell leanings after all. I knew that her brother had a soft spot for the holidays, despite his trucker machismo, but Emma? Well, at least she had volunteered to help. I clung to the thought.

"I'll call Sheila today and get the skinny, then track down that maid of honor. Don't worry, Momma. It'll be fine."

Her confidence buoyed my spirits, and I went about my morning routine with a lighter heart.

Twenty minutes later, I crossed the Silas Deane Highway and entered Wethersfield's historic district on Old Main Street. I might not work here at the moment, but starting my day without coffee from the Village Diner was unthinkable. A sign announcing that the town had been established in 1634 alerted me to the change in ambience that waited around the first curve. Almost immediately, the morning traffic sounds dropped away. The few remaining cars were relatively easy to ignore. The houses occupying the first few blocks, circa 1940, quickly gave way to far older structures. Once past Garden Street, I was plunged into the nineteenth century, then the eighteenth, as plaques next to weathered front doors announced each house's vintage. Finally, discreet signage approved by the local historic commission directed visitors to the museums and homesteads of particular significance.

Interspersed with these august structures were the various establishments that made up the Old Wethersfield business district. I experienced a brief pang as I drove by the Law Barn, which until recently had housed MACK Realty and my daughter Emma's place of employment. Emma, a real estate paralegal, and her lawyer boss Isabel had responded to the market slide by downsizing to a two-person office in Glastonbury. Now a Space to Let sign swung forlornly in the chilly breeze outside the empty building. After that came Blades Salon, Antiques on Main,

Mainly Tea, the Webb-Deane-Stevens Museum, and an assortment of small businesses, including a travel agency, bakery and the Village Diner.

Parking along Old Main Street could be difficult later in the day, but finding a spot was easy at this hour. I snugged the Jetta against the curb and dashed into the diner, where the mingled aromas of hot coffee and cinnamon something washed over me. Deenie, the chronically harassed college student who filled all of the diner's take-out orders during the morning shift, greeted me. "Morning, Kate. Just coffee, or is this an off-your-diet day? The sticky buns are nice and fresh."

As often as not, I gave in to temptation, but not this morning. "Just coffee today, Deenie. Don't want to be late for my new job."

She grinned at me and went to fill a large paper cup with the diner's special brew. "Yeah, I heard Sister Marguerite talked you into helping out with the UCC fundraiser this year. A big to-do at the Wadsworth, visit from Santa and all that, isn't it? Better you than me. I helped out with that a couple of years ago. All those lah-de-dah women expecting to be treated like royalty." She rolled her eyes while I tried not to look discomfited. Sister Marguerite had omitted any mention of egocentric donors. I smiled weakly and handed Deenie the exact amount, which I knew from long experience.

"Well, it's only for a couple of weeks. How bad could it be?" I made a hasty exit before she could tell me.

Today's priority was a full run-through of Thursday evening's event. Despite the surface confusion of yesterday's meeting, I felt certain that the chaos had been organized. After all, this wasn't the first such fundraiser these people had orchestrated. They had been through it all before, probably dozens of times. No doubt my own unfamiliarity with the proceedings had been the source of my misgivings. I would get up to speed this morning.

Accordingly, I parked and locked the Jetta a bit closer to the Cathedral than I had the previous morning and joined the parade of volunteers moving purposefully through a rear entrance to St. Joseph's and into the lower church. I looked around curiously. To my untutored eyes, even this lower space looked pretty grand. Row after row of pews were interspersed with wide aisles. A full altar stood at the front of the space, and a smaller, separate seating area occupied the space to the right. A simple altar and what looked to be a baptismal font were located there. The main nave upstairs with its towering ceiling and huge, stained glass windows must be dazzling. At some point, I hoped to glimpse the world-renowned pipe organ, dubbed "The Mighty Austin," that distinguished musicians flocked to play in a series of concerts offered by the Cathedral throughout the year.

I watched parishioners dipping their fingers into bowls of holy water, then crossing themselves in the age-old Catholic ritual. My lack of participation seemed to cause no consternation, and I soon realized that I had plenty of non-Catholic company among the volunteers. Apparently, this meeting was as ecumenical as the UCC itself. I knew that previous meetings had been held at other churches and synagogues throughout the region.

"Okay, boys and girls, let's get this show on the road." Sister Marguerite addressed the group of perhaps fifty with her customary lack of pretense. "Shirley, who called this meeting, and what are we supposed to be doing again?" Her little joke drew appreciative chuckles. Then the staff and volunteers fell silent and prepared to concentrate.

"As you've probably noticed, we're missing a few folks today. This year's strain of flu has begun eating into our numbers, and from the coughing and sniffling I'm hearing out there, I'm very much afraid that we'll be down a few more by tomorrow." We looked around nervously. I had indeed heard the phlegmy evidence of contagious virus and shrank instinctively a bit farther from my pew-mates. The last thing I needed at this moment was the flu. "So the first order of business is to recruit more volunteers. We can't have our prestigious guests scavenging for food and drink at the buffet table tomorrow evening. We need wait-staff to pass things around and charm the money out of their pockets. If you have any friends or relatives available, get them on the phone as soon as we adjourn and line 'em up."

Immediately, I thought of Margo and Strutter. We were meeting for dinner this very evening, and I would beg for their help on Sister Marguerite's behalf. Strutter was already acquainted with James O'Halloran, having sold him and his wife a house a couple of years ago, and Margo ... well, Margo was always up for a good time, even if she had to pass a few canapés in the process. As for beguiling the guests, my partners were unsurpassed in that area. I made a note.

An hour later, we had been given our marching orders and dispersed as quickly as we had gathered. The schedule for Thursday evening had been confirmed, and each person in the room had his or her role down pat. As I had suspected, this was old hat to most of these folks. Because the Atheneum would already be decorated to the hilt with the fabulous trees, wreaths, and more whimsical decorations of the season contributed by organizations throughout Greater Hartford to support the Atheneum's own fundraising efforts, the UCC would have to add little to the ambience. A committee of experienced decorators would add the final touches to the refreshment tables early in the day.

By mid-afternoon, all of the auction and raffle prizes would be artfully displayed along a long wall near the open bar. "Ladle the punch liberally, remember," Sister Marguerite admonished. "Show them a good time, and their wallets will practically fall open by themselves. But keep a close eye on them as they head out the door. Our famous Christmas punch is well spiked, and we don't want to send any inebriates out into the streets. Just call Jimmy's Cab Service, and he'll send around one of his boys to drive the over-enthusiastic imbibers home safely."

At five-thirty, the doors would officially open, and platters of mouth-watering hors d'oeuvres would be circulated by the volunteer waiters. A popular senior citizens chorus would provide twenty minutes of seasonal selections, ending with "Here Comes Santa Claus." This was the cue for James O'Halloran, in full Santa Claus regalia, to make his entrance and distribute the goody bags which had already been packed into a large sack that would be smuggled into the Wadsworth well ahead of time.

"It's crazy and chaotic, but somehow I have confidence that we'll pull this off," I told Armando on the phone after work. At the sight of me coming into the living room, Jasmine perked up, but when she realized Armando wasn't behind me, she sighed and dropped her chin back onto her front paws. Her eyes were half open, and she looked, well, sad.

As if reading my mind, Armando asked, "How is Jasmine doing?" The two had formed such a strong emotional attachment to each other since Armando had moved in the previous autumn, Jasmine had all but abandoned me. I was okay for the mundane caregiver duties such as feeding and litter box cleaning, but she chose to spend her true quality time with Armando. This was facilitated by our separate-bedroom arrangement, which we had agreed was absolutely necessary for middle-aged, stuck-in-our ways housemates. For the last year,

Jasmine had spent her nights sleeping in the crook of Armando's arm, thriving under his gentle stroking, while Simon, growing slowly weaker and sicker from kidney and thyroid ailments, had nestled close to me under the covers.

"She's okay physically," I told Armando now, "but I think she's depressed. Losing Simon was bad enough, but now that you're gone ..." I changed gears, not wanting to distress him. "Anyway, she's sitting right here next to me. Guess she figures I'm better than nothing. So how are things going there?"

Quickly, he filled me in. Then, "I am sorry to have to cut our conversation short, *Mia*, but there is a working dinner this evening, and I must go now to get there on time." I rolled my eyes. Promptness was not one of Armando's strong points. "We will speak again tomorrow. So, do you have big plans while I am safely out of the way?"

"As a matter of fact, I have a dinner date of my own," I teased him, "with Margo and Strutter. It seems like forever since I've seen them. When we all worked together, it was easy to keep up with each other's lives, but now I feel as if we're drifting apart."

Although I knew he understood my melancholy, Armando had little time to reassure me. "That will change, you know that. This downfalling in the real estate market cannot last forever." Despite twenty years in the U.S., Armando still had a little trouble with English idioms.

"I know, you're right. We'll all be back together soon, chatting up a storm over morning coffee. Besides, I plan to rope them into helping with the gala tomorrow night. So run along and make some money. One of us has to be steadily employed." I made kissing noises and disconnected. "Well, old girl, how does some water-packed tuna fish sound for your dinner?" Apparently, the proposed menu didn't appeal to Jasmine as much as sleeping, and once again her eyelids drooped shut. I made a mental note to try to tempt her appetite again before bedtime and went off to meet my friends for dinner.

The early crowd at Vito's was in full swing, but Margo and Strutter had saved me a seat at the small bar in the front room. Despite her relatively casual attire, Margo was the epitome of chic, blonde elegance, and Strutter's darker Jamaican beauty glowed in the dim overhead lighting. Each of them routinely lit up any room she was in, but together, they were amazing. I smiled at the sight of them, and they seemed just as glad to see me. It had been too long.

"Married life seems to be agreeing with you," I observed, giving Margo a quick hug. The previous New Year's Eve, she had married Wethersfield's handsome chief of homicide, John Harkness, changing his entire demeanor from dour to dynamic. Though we would never express it to Margo, our fear had been that just one man, even one as impressive as Lieutenant Harkness, wouldn't be able to sustain the interest of our libidinous Southern belle, but so far, she all but purred with contentment. "How is your gorgeous new daughter?" I greeted Strutter before hopping onto the barstool they had saved between them. Margo ordered me a glass of shiraz, and Strutter wasted no time producing a handful of photos of baby Olivia, who had arrived late last spring to the delight of her husband, another John, and her thirteen-year-old son Charlie, the only good thing that had come from a disastrous early liaison.

"Not just gorgeous," Strutter amended as Margo hung over my shoulder to get a look. "I can already tell this girl is going to be hell on wheels, smart and funny and manipulative, whoooeee! Just like Emma but with a better tan," she winked at me. "She has had my husband and son eating out of her hand since they first laid eyes on her, and do you know? She's already pushing with those fat little legs to stand up. I am in such trouble." She grinned to let us know she didn't really mind.

Margo wasn't a baby person, nor was I, but we couldn't help but enjoy our friend's obvious pride in her new offspring. Early in her pregnancy Strutter had been worried that her new husband, who was in his early fifties, wouldn't welcome a new arrival. He soon set her straight, and from that point on, Olivia may have set a new record for being the most eagerly anticipated baby in Connecticut.

"It's for certain that girl is goin' to break more than a few hearts," Margo observed. "Takes right after her mama with those big, blue eyes and dimples and that amazin'

milk chocolate complexion. Makes me regret bein'
Caucasian. Think she'll be able to master that hip-swingin'
sashay of yours?" Strutter's sexy walk was the reason
behind her sobriquet.

"Don't you worry. It's a Jamaican thing. It's in our
genes," Strutter assured her. She returned the photos to
her purse with a final pat. "So what's going on with you
two?"

We carried our glasses into the main dining area and
secured a booth at the back, the better to catch up on each
other's lives. By the time our orders arrived, we had pretty
well covered the progress of sales at Vista View, the
retirement community our realty firm still represented,
albeit from Margo's living room these days; Margo's
blissful adjustment to married life with her handsome
police lieutenant; and Strutter's consternation at how
much she had forgotten about dealing with an infant, let
alone the challenges presented by her son Charlie, now a
teenager. "So how are you and Armando managing under
the same roof?" Strutter wanted to know. "Is the
honeymoon over?"

After five years of dating, Armando and I had moved
in together a little more than a year ago. To everyone's
amazement, including our own, neither of us had yet
killed the other. We had known going in that however
much we loved each other, the fact that we were both
strong-willed, independent, middle-aged adults who had
enjoyed our own spaces for more than a decade apiece
would call for a major adjustment.

"I'm not saying we haven't had a spat or two," I began, but Margo snorted into her wineglass. It was one of her less attractive mannerisms, since it usually signaled her complete disavowal of whatever I was saying.

"Knock down, drag out fights, would be more accurate," she contradicted me now, and Strutter giggled. "We lived through them with you, remember?"

"Okay, okay," I capitulated, "a couple of yelling matches, maybe, but it never got physical. It's not easy living with a man again after all these years, especially a Colombian packrat whose relationship with time is entirely different than mine."

"We're with you about livin' with a man, Sugar, but you're on your own with the packrat who's always late thing," Margo compromised, and Strutter nodded her agreement. The two of them would make a compelling argument for matrimony. Margo, who had been not-so-discreetly lascivious for as long as I'd know her exuded contentment with her role as Mrs. John Harkness, and new mother Strutter, all shiny eyed and glowing, was the picture of domesticated bliss. She munched thoughtfully on a mouthful of pizza.

"How are things going with the new job?"

"Temporary job," I corrected her swiftly. "I'm so glad you asked." Between mouthfuls of my excellent chicken Caesar salad, I filled them in on the happenings at the UCC and the plans for the fundraiser at the Wadsworth the following evening. "I'm telling you, I have a whole new respect for people who raise money for a living. It was tough enough before the economy hit the skids, but now everyone has to work twice as hard just to keep basic services afloat. The commitment of these people is simply amazing, and they do it for salaries that would make our old legal secretarial pay look like casino jackpots."

A few years back, the three of us had worked at a prestigious law firm supporting some of the rudest, crudest, most expensive attorneys in the business. Our shared disenchantment had prompted us to leave the firm and open MACK Realty.

"It has to be tough," Strutter agreed. "Is the gala at the Wadsworth coming together?"

"Despite all odds, it is, but as of today we have a new problem. The flu has taken out a dozen or so of our volunteer wait staff, with who knows how many more to follow in the next twenty-four hours." I grinned at my best friends in the world, who surely knew what was coming. "So what are your plans for tomorrow evening?"

"Ooooh, really?" Margo squealed. "You know there's just nothin' in the world I enjoy more than rubbin' elbows with the filthy rich." Then she narrowed her eyes, suddenly suspicious. "What's the catch? Do I have to hide in the kitchen and wash dishes?"

Strutter laughed. "She'll probably have us slaving away over a hot dishpan all night, and we won't get so much as a glimpse of the movers and shakers."

I widened my eyes. "Would I do that to you?" They both nodded vigorously. "Let me rephrase that. Would I do that to you on just one day's notice? Now that would truly not be nice."

Strutter helped herself to more pizza. Margo took a sip of wine and arched an eyebrow. "Okay, I'll spell it out. All you have to do is show up an hour ahead of time wearing black pants and a white blouse. A fancy caterer will shove silver trays loaded with to-die-for canapés at you and send you into the main room to circulate. You can have all the free samples you want. Open bar. No dishwashing." I waited. "Would you like that in writing?"

Big grins. "I'm in," Strutter answered. "John and Charlie can take over babysitting duties for a while. I just hope I still remember how to make conversation with adults." I was delighted for the UCC and for Strutter. If new motherhood was still anything like it used to be, she could use a night out, and this promised to be an interesting evening for all of us.

"Me too, Darlin'," Margo agreed. "At least this time, you're not draggin' us into a murder investigation."

 **Three**

Although I'm not a religious person, I really don't object to Christmas in principle, I reflected as I dodged through the morning commuter traffic on Thursday. In fact, I enjoy the holiday in small doses. I'm especially partial to the decorations and music that accompany the season. I don't even object to the exchange of gifts within reason. My dread springs from the early years of my marriage. I hated having Christmas shoved down my throat not only by the media and the retail establishment, but also by my Midwestern in-laws who were a part of the package deal when I married Michael.

Left to my own devices, I actually would have enjoyed celebrating the season with Emma and Joey, introducing them to the spirit of the holiday through books, music, playing Secret Santa, exchanging small gifts, decorating, and maybe even doing some modest entertaining. It was the relentlessness of the thing that got my back up. It seemed as though everything from late October through early January was focused on buying, consuming, and attending things related to the omnipresent holiday, as if it were somehow un-American to turn one's thoughts elsewhere for the duration.

Michael's family was large and gregarious, and their holiday gatherings were both ritualistic and unavoidable. Early on, I had been labeled the family Grinch, but I found nothing enjoyable about joining more than thirty of Michael's family members in his mother's overheated four-room apartment at the end of what had already been an exhausting Christmas Day. The year I found myself huddled underneath my mother-in-law's dining room table, knees pulled under my chin to avoid having my feet stepped on by sugared-up, semi-hysterical children, I vowed that it was my last appearance at the annual horror. It was also the beginning of the end of our marriage, but then, hindsight is always twenty-twenty.

After a hiatus of many years following my relatively amicable divorce from Michael, I had settled into what was for me an acceptable level of festivity. It included a very few holiday gatherings, about forty-eight hours of Christmas music, and a Christmas Eve buffet in front of the fireplace in the company of whoever cared to drop by. In recent years, Emma and Joey, accompanied by ever-changing boyfriends and girlfriends, had spent the evening with me and Armando, whom they had accepted as a member of their extended family. Sometimes my sister, who had moved to the Midwest a few years back, came for a visit, as did one or another of the kids' friends who were in the area visiting family. We ate all of our favorite foods, drank good wine, and played cut-throat games of Trivial Pursuit, Uno, and even poker. The evening's big winner had the privilege of designating which charity would be awarded the consolidated winnings.

In my opinion, it was perfect. Emma and Joey were denied nothing, since they enjoyed a traditional Christmas Day with their father, his second wife Sheila, and dozens of their family members. They exchanged a great number of expensive gifts, then tucked into an outrageous sit-down dinner, while Armando and I enjoyed the peace and quiet of Christmas afternoon.

The system worked beautifully, and I saw no reason to change it until Michael's surprising telephone call. Not only was I now attempting to coordinate a massive fundraising event and staging a traditional Christmas Eve for Emma's new boyfriend, I was expected to host a post-Christmas wedding, all without Armando's calming influence to keep me on an even keel. A pang of loneliness stabbed me as I merged into the traffic pattern around Pulaski Circle and negotiated the rest of my route to the UCC office with the growing confidence of an experienced commuter, despite the SUV jockey glued to my back bumper.

Somehow, the peace and solitude of my condo weren't nearly as appealing as they had been a week ago. Even Jasmine seemed even more lethargic without Armando, if that was possible. At least Margo and Strutter would be on hand to offer moral support this evening. It was a cheering thought.

The morning passed in a blur of pre-party jitters as everyone checked and double-checked their preparations. Four more volunteer waiters and waitresses had succumbed to the flu overnight, but enough replacements had been recruited to make do with some last-minute juggling of assignments. Strutter had been assigned to hospitality and check-in duty at the Atheneum Square North entrance, where her natural warmth and stunning good looks would make a wonderful first impression. Margo would be pleased with her assignment to circulate among the guests bearing a silver tray filled with cups of the champagne punch to which Sister Marguerite had referred.

By three o'clock, the entire staff had migrated to the Wadsworth. Even the Grinch-iest among us couldn't help but be impressed by the ambience. Although there was no snow on the ground as yet, the lowering clouds made for an early dusk. We had not yet had a significant snowfall in Connecticut, but tonight might just be the night. Instead of dampening our spirits, the gloom outdoors contrasted appealingly with the warmth and glittering lights inside the beautiful old structure. The overall impression was one of festivity and elegance, which was precisely the note we had hoped to strike.

I had not had an opportunity to visit the Wadsworth in a couple of years, so I slipped away from the others to familiarize myself with the layout of the area we would be using during the course of the evening. It was all on the first floor, and the main exhibit areas would be safely

locked away from wandering visitors. Although the main
museum entrance was on Main Street, that would be
closed at 4:30 p.m. to minimize security risks.

All of the invited guests had been instructed to park on
the surrounding streets and enter the Museum from
Atheneum Square North. The Avery Lobby was there,
along with a coatroom which contained several portable
wheelchairs for the use of Museum patrons. I doubted that
we would need any of those this evening, but one never
knew. The entrance to the Museum's movie theater, which
was located on the basement level, was next to the
coatroom but was roped off for the occasion. No need to
risk having a tipsy guest take a tumble down the stairs.

The Avery Lobby opened directly into a large hall,
which was where the bulk of the evening's activities
would take place. A large fountain in the center provided a
dramatic focal point, and a dazzling array of trees,
painstakingly decorated and donated by local
organizations for the museum's silent auction, occupied
every space inch of wall space. The only exception was a
raised platform in one corner, where a chamber ensemble
from the University of Hartford's acclaimed Hartt School
of Music would provide background music.

Late in the afternoon, I took my black hostess trousers
and white silk shirt with me to the women's room in order
to change in one of the stalls. It must have been a popular
idea, because a short line had formed outside the door. In a
niche across the hall I noticed a door marked Women's
Committee office and decided to use it as a makeshift

dressing room. I tapped once on the door and ducked inside, not expecting anyone to be occupying it.

"Oh! You startled me." A plump and pretty brunette whirled from behind a miniscule desk, where she was holding together the half-buttoned front of a gauzy cocktail dress with one hand. "Guess I shouldn't be using the office as a changing room, but there's a line outside the loo. Come in, come in. The least I could have done was lock the door." She extended her free hand. "Mary O'Halloran."

I closed the door quickly and squeezed her hand in return. "Kate Lawrence. I'm helping out at the UCC while Sister Marguerite's assistant is on maternity leave. You must be James' wife. I believe you know my business partner, Strutter ... uh, Charlene Putnam. James tells me that she represented the seller of the house you and he bought in Wethersfield a few years back."

Mary fastened her top button and smoothed the burgundy frock over her full hips, wrinkling her brow in thought. "Charlene, Charlene. Why, yes! She was the gorgeous young woman with the dazzling blue eyes and the West Indies lilt. So nice, too. You work together?"

"Not so much recently. Our real estate firm, MACK Realty, has been reduced to a skeleton crew until the market picks back up, but yes, she's my partner."

"Strutter, huh?" Mary twinkled. "Very appropriate, now that I remember that outrageous walk of hers."

I returned her smile. "You caught me. I'm usually a little more circumspect with new acquaintances. You'll see her later, as a matter of fact, along with our third partner, Margo Harkness. The flu has claimed so many victims this week, I had to recruit Strutter and Margo to help out tonight. You're right about that line outside the women's room, by the way. Do you mind if I do a quick change in here, too?"

"Be my guest. In fact, I'll leave you in peace to do it. I was due to check in with the caterers five minutes ago, and knowing Henri, he's in a swivet wondering where I am. Then I have to find James and help him into his Santa suit. He can never quite manage the padding." She bustled around the desk, and I took her place.

"*Henri?* Sounds fancy schmancy."

Mary giggled. "It's plain Henry Kozlowski from East Hartford, actually, but that doesn't quite fit in with his upscale professional image these days. I waited for her to scoot through the door before I pulled my sweater over my head, but instead of leaving, she fidgeted once again with the buttons on her dress. Her merry expression had faded, and she appeared lost in thought. I couldn't help but notice the worry lines etched between her eyebrows.

"Anything I can help you out with?" I prodded tentatively.

"Oh, sorry. I'm a bit distracted is all. James' brother Joseph is in town unexpectedly." She sighed. "His visits are always unexpected. Now that I think of it, we haven't seen Joseph in probably eight or nine years. He and James don't get along, you see," she confided.

"I'm sorry," I sympathized. "Relatives can be trying at

the best of times, but the hectic holidays are no time for a surprise visit."

"Mmmm, you're right. It's a family thing. Joseph is the bad penny that keeps turning up, but only when he wants something. We just don't know what it is this time." She gave herself a little shake. "No doubt we'll find out soon enough, so it's silly to waste time worrying about it now. James has spent his entire life getting Joseph out of hot water, and he'll take care of whatever the problem is this time, too, but not tonight."

"Every family has at least one," I agreed. "You're smart to be able to put Joseph on the back burner."

"James works so hard, and he looks forward to playing Santa Claus all year long. I mustn't let anything spoil it, not even Joseph. See you later." She waggled her fingers at me and vanished into the hallway.

A few minutes later I had changed into my black pants and white shirt and had freshened my make-up with the aid of the compact I kept in my purse. I wrapped my handbag inside my work clothes and stuffed the whole bundle under the desk, hoping I would remember where I'd left everything a few hours hence. I snapped off the light and opened the office door to scout the hallway. The coast was clear, so I slipped out and closed the door quietly behind me, wondering what the evening held in store.

It didn't take long to locate Margo and Strutter. It was no

surprise to me that they were the center of attention
among the volunteer waiters and waitresses who had
gathered in the Avery Court to receive assignments from
Henri/Henry. The sight of my two lovely friends, one
sleekly blonde and groomed to a fare-thee-well, the other
glowing and dimpled, warmed my heart. *How many other
people would drop everything on less than twenty-four hours'
notice and rush to help out at a charity function?* I wondered.
Then I looked around at the dozens of willing workers.
More than I would have thought a week ago, apparently.

Strutter caught my eye and blew me a kiss before
scurrying off to the Avery Lobby with one of the security
guards. I waved and hoped that the stylish little faux fur
wrap over her shoulders would protect her from the chilly
drafts that would inevitably accompany the opening and
closing door. The last thing a new mother needs is a head
cold. Margo finished flirting with the half-dozen young
men who had already clustered around her and winked at
me. She accepted a tray of hors d'oeuvres from a harried
supervisor who shooed her into the waiting crowd.

I trailed along behind the line of wait staff making their
way into the main exhibition areas. The display was
absolutely smashing with thousands of lights on the
donated trees twinkling and gleaming. A *Who's Who* of
Hartford's elite, dressed to impress in jewel tones for the
holiday, circulated among them, while the Hartt School
musicians supplied elegant background music. Although it
was not yet five-thirty, the crowd was already impressive.
Every UCC staff member who passed me paused to point

out State Representative So-and-So standing over by the entrance and Mr. and Mrs. Something-or-Other, who owned half of the commercial real estate in the city, chatting with the mayor by the musicians.

Every few minutes Sister Marguerite whirled by on her way to pay homage to one or another of the distinguished guests. Despite what had to have been a grueling day, she looked animated and elegant in her gray silk cocktail suit, if a nun could be said to wear such a garment, and low-heeled black pumps. I was grateful that my wide-legged hostess britches flowed all the way to the floor, nicely concealing my comfy ballet slippers. About two hours in high heels is my limit.

By six-thirty, the auction had begun. The guest auctioneer was a popular weatherman from a local television station, and he was really working the crowd. I had never seen so many people have such a good time spending money. Lois Billard and her volunteer crew were kept busy accepting large donations and distributing claim checks for merchandise to be collected later.

Since everything seemed to be going according to plan refreshment-wise, I decided to check up on Santa Claus. I wormed my way through the crush being careful not to jostle the expensively clad assemblage holding cups of Henri's famous holiday punch. The precise recipe was a closely guarded secret, but as someone had described it to me, "it packs a wallop." I looked forward to sampling it myself a bit later in the evening. Judging from the rising volume of conversation, the brew was working its magic. I could only hope it would loosen the party-goers' grip on their wallets as well it seemed to be loosening their tongues.

I wondered how soon Santa's official visit was due to occur. Mary was nowhere to be seen, so I headed toward the Office of Museum Education, where the wait staff went to refill their pitchers, to check on progress with James. Halfway across the room, I was startled to see James himself in front of me, heading purposefully in the same direction. The small bald spot at the crown of his head stabbed me to the heart. It reminded me of the one I hadn't yet had the heart to tell Armando about. We're better off not knowing some things about ourselves until we have to, I had decided. Besides, I found it rather endearing.

James was still not in costume. Pausing at the door, he looked left, then right, almost furtively before yanking open the door and insinuating himself inside. I was puzzled by the furtiveness of his movements until I realized that Santa's true identity was probably kept secret. Only the UCC staff would be in the know.

It was doubtful that James would appreciate company while he got into his ensemble, so I changed direction and headed to the Avery Lobby, where things were relatively peaceful. Although there would doubtless be late arrivals, the bulk of the invited guests had already been admitted. The bulging coat racks opposite the guard desk attested to the wintry nip in the air, but that only added to the seasonal festivity.

"How are things going?" I greeted Strutter, who was

resting her feet while she could by sitting at the desk next to the guard on duty.

"All quiet here for the moment. Kate, I'd like you to meet Luis Gomez." She gestured toward the young man at her left. "He was recruited to help out at the last minute just like I was. The flu has invaded the Wadsworth's security staff, too."

"Hi, Luis." I held out my hand. "Kate Lawrence, temporary worker at the UCC. Any excitement so far? Inebriated guests? Lost earrings? Forgotten invitations?"

"No, Ma'am, not so far, but it's early yet, so I'm still hoping for some excitement." He returned my grin.

"Good thing we have this guest list, though." Strutter patted the pages spread out before them on the desk. "So many of us are new to this group, we wouldn't have a clue who should be admitted without it."

I scanned the list. A number of the names were vaguely familiar, but I wouldn't be able to pick out their faces in the crowd. A checkmark next to the name indicated that an invited guest had, in fact, shown up, information that would affect his or her inclusion on future invitation lists.

"Why are there two checkmarks next to James Halloran's name?" I wondered.

Strutter peered at the list and shrugged. "Must have gone out and come back in again. Some of them do that, mostly the smokers." She pointed out another double-checked name. "Listen, Girlfriend, do you think you could send a waiter along with some of those fabulous canapés?

Luis and I are wasting away."

"Oh, I'm so sorry!" I apologized and sprang for the door. "Here the rest of us are absolutely wallowing in food and drink, and you two are stuck out here starving. I'll be back in two shakes."

Ten minutes later, having fortified my colleagues with plates heaped high with Henry/Henri's specialties, I was pleased to hear the musicians signaling Santa's arrival with an elegant rendition of "Here Comes Santa Claus." I scurried back into the main room to secure a good vantage point from which to watch the fun. Having finally shaken her entourage of young admirers, Margo was taking a break in the shelter of the ornate trees flanking the bandstand, and I crossed the room to join her.

"Hey, Lady," I greeted her. "How's the refreshment biz?"

"Hard on the feet but otherwise fine," she rejoined. I noticed that her feet were bare and looked around for the strappy sandals in which she had begun the evening. She pointed to the lowest branch of the tree behind her, where her silver sandals dangled merrily. "Is your CFO person ready to do the Santa thing?"

"James O'Halloran, and yes, I believe this is it." We looked around expectantly as the musicians paused, then swung into a repeat performance of "Here Comes Santa Claus." An anticipatory hush fell over the room, but no Santa appeared. I noticed Sister Marguerite waving frantically at me from the other side of the bandstand and excused my way through the crowd to join her.

"Something must have gone wrong with his costume," she whispered in my ear. Be a dear and nip over to the Education Office and see what's what. I'll have to jolly these people along with an announcement of some kind." I nodded to show I understood and retraced my steps through the crowd, signaling Margo to join me. Sister stepped onto the bandstand and approached the microphone. "Looks like Santa's been delayed, Folks. Something about a city ordinance forbidding reindeer landings on public buildings, but we'll have it sorted out in a few moments. Until then, please continue to enjoy our hospitality," I heard her address the assemblage.

While the crowd was thus distracted, we made a dash for the Museum Office. Before I had a chance to knock, the door flew open, and Mary O'Halloran yanked me inside, followed closely by Margo.

"Where's James?" Mary and I demanded of each other simultaneously, looking around the room a bit wildly. The caterer's supplies were stacked everywhere, and a great heap of small, wrapped packages spilled from one corner. A huge, stainless steel vat of Henri's punch sat on the floor, a plastic pitcher floating aimlessly in the middle. The waiters refilling their trays of cups must have been in a hurry, as repeated splashing had formed puddles around the container. I wondered at the sanitation of this arrangement, but then I supposed the alcohol in the punch would kill off any germs.

"Looks like Santa had other places to be this evenin'," Margo observed, then added practically, "Will anyone else fit into the costume?"

"What costume? I don't even see that. James was headed this way nearly an hour ago," I said, genuinely puzzled now. "I remember that it seemed late for him not to be in costume, but I know he came into this room. I saw him go through the door, and all the presents for the guests that were in his big sack are piled over there in the corner. Do you suppose he was taken ill all of a sudden? The flu has been going through the UCC like wildfire."

"Oh, dear," Mary wailed softly. "He wasn't feeling very well this afternoon, but I told him he'd feel better once he was here. When I came to help him into his Santa suit after you and I talked, Kate, he wasn't here, but I just thought he was in the men's room or something." She looked forlorn. "Where on earth can he be? I know. I'll call his cell phone. He always has that on him." She rushed out of the room in search of a telephone.

"Now what?" I asked Margo, at a loss. I picked up the corner of the paper cloth that covered the one steel table in the room and peered underneath. Nothing. "The packages are here, but Santa's toy sack isn't. Oh, this is not good. Sister Marguerite is going to be apoplectic," I added half to myself, but there was nothing for it but to go out there and give the good Sister the facts.

"Tell you what. Before you give Sister Marguerite the bad news, let's tiptoe out to the lobby and see if Strutter has seen Santa or his toy sack. If not, we'll just have to come up with a Plan B." She winked to reassure me, and I followed her back to the main hall, where the crowd seemed a bit subdued but still game. As discreetly as possible, we made our way along the walls to the Avery Lobby, where Strutter was bursting to know what was going on.

"That's what we're here to ask you. Have you seen James O'Halloran, the fellow who was supposed to be playing Santa Claus tonight? He was one of those double-checked names we were looking at earlier on the guest list."

Strutter crossed her eyes at me in disgust. "I think I would have remembered Santa Claus blowing past, with or without reindeer. If O'Halloran went out for a smoke, he didn't do it in costume." She looked at Luis for confirmation. He looked nonplussed.

"Ummm, well ... O'Halloran actually did come through here," he finally admitted, blushing to the roots of his buzz cut. "I remembered after we were talking about the double check marks next to his name. He wasn't in costume or anything. He asked me where we kept the wheelchairs. Said it would be a lot easier to get his bag of presents into position if he had something with wheels to move it around in. So I pointed him to that closet over there behind the coat racks, and he disappeared for a minute. You were in the women's room," he added for Strutter's benefit.

"Oh, yeah," she muttered, remembering.

"Right about then, a big group came in, and I was busy checking them off and so on. A few minutes later, O'Halloran came back pushing a big sack in the wheelchair. Went right out that door."

"Did he come back in again? Did you put a third checkmark next to his name?"

"That's what I can't remember, Ma'am. I honestly think I would recall doing it myself, but I just don't."

We looked at each other. "Would you know if one of the wheelchairs was still missing?" Margo asked finally.

Poor Luis turned even redder. "No, Ma'am, I would not. This is my first time here, and the wheelchairs move back and forth from the Main Street entrance to this one, as I understand it. People pick one up where they come in and drop it off wherever they exit the building."

"Looks like Santa flew the coop," I stated the obvious.

"Vamoosed," Strutter agreed.

"Blew this pop-stand," Margo offered. "Before your time, Darlin'," she told Luis, who looked confused.

Since we couldn't think of anything more productive to do, we all trooped over to the coat room. Luis flipped on the light. Four wheelchairs were propped neatly against the wall, which gave us no information at all, since we had no idea how many had been there at the beginning of the evening. "What's that?" Strutter bent over and peered at a wet trail on the floor. It led into and out of the coat room. Luis dropped to a crouch and swiped at it with a finger.

"It's sticky," he reported. "I think it's some of that punch the waiters have been passing around all evening. Look, it goes all the way to the outer doors." We looked.

I remembered Sister Marguerite and the three hundred guests awaiting Santa Claus in vain. "Okay, first things first. Luis, you're going to have to man the desk by yourself for a while. Get a message to me if you see O'Halloran come in or out." He hastened back to his station. "Strutter, I need you to check the rest of this floor for signs of James O'Halloran. Middle-aged, medium height, glasses."

"You just described ninety percent of the men in this room, Sugar," Margo pointed out.

I thought for a moment. "Okay, he has a little bald spot on the back of his head. If you can't find him, look for his wife Mary. Pretty brunette with some gray at the front, attractively plump, wine-colored dress that buttons up the front."

"Yes, Ma'am!" Strutter saluted sharply and scooted for the main room.

"Margo," I grabbed her sleeve urgently. "I want you to find that caterer and charm him into performing a miracle. We need every waiter and waitress in this place to return to the staging area, off-load their refreshments, and fill their trays with those gifts piled in the corner. When they hear Sister Marguerite give them a cue, they're to sweep into the main hall and distribute the gifts. Got it?"

"No problem, Darlin'," and I knew that for Margo, it would not be. Charm was her middle name. "What will the cue be?"

"Damned if I know at the moment, but you'll recognize it when you hear it," I assured her. "Now I get the fun job of breaking the news to a very tired nun who's already had one heck of a day that her star performer is among the missing. Go! Go!" I pushed Margo through the doors ahead of me and went to find Sister Marguerite.

 **Four**

By nine-thirty the party was over, and by ten-fifteen, a casual observer would have been unaware that one had even occurred. After a full day of preparation and hours on their feet, the caterer's staff had removed every remnant of food and drink and wiped and mopped their way out the door. Henry Kozlowski had been the hero of the evening. Within ten minutes of our discovery that Santa was among the missing, he had marshaled his ragtag and largely untrained troops, heaped their trays with presents for our generous guests, and lined them up by twos at the entrance to the Avery Court. On his cue, the ambient lighting was dimmed, and two volunteers bearing battery-powered candles led the gift-bearers as they swept magnificently into the hall to appreciative *ooohs* and *ahhhhs*. At that moment, Henry became every inch Henri in my mind. The man had true class, the kind that counted when the chips were down.

I thanked Margo and Strutter until they held up their hands in protest. "We absolutely could not have pulled this off without you two," I gushed for the tenth time as they gathered their purses and car keys and headed for the door.

"I wouldn't have missed it, Sugar," Margo assured me, still the picture of pulled-together perfection after all that had transpired, but I had noticed her wincing as she stuffed her tired feet back into the silver sandals

"Just remember to let us know what happened to Santa," Strutter added, tucking a box of scrumptious leftovers into her oversized handbag. "Charlie and John are just going to love these goodies."

"You're the best!" I called after them, and they fled through the lobby, where a weary Luis let them out onto Atheneum Square North, then locked the door behind them.

I walked slowly through the nearly deserted exhibition hall to the Women's Committee office to retrieve my own coat and purse. This time, the door to the little room stood open. Lois Billard and the assistant financial officer of the UCC, a retired corporate comptroller, huddled with Sister Marguerite at the desk. In the absence of the CFO, they were uncertain of the legal protocol that applied to the counting and reporting of auction proceeds.

"'Tis no fault of his own, I'm sure," said Sister Marguerite, "but James' absence does make things a bit dicey."

"As long as we log in all of the proceeds together, which means counting and recounting for verification, I think we'll be okay," the assistant opined, "but it can't wait until tomorrow. Of that much, I'm sure. We'll have to do it right here, tonight, then sign and date some sort of document saying we all agree on how much we got from whom and for what." Lois and Sister both groaned.

"Can I help?" I offered, hoping against hope that they would decline. I was dead on my feet.

"No, no, Katie girl," Sister shooed me on my way. "You're wonderful to offer, but at this point, that would just make too many cooks in the kitchen. Off you go, now, and we'll see you tomorrow, though a bit later than usual," she predicted.

"Why are you in California? Why aren't you here?" I whined at Armando via long distance. It was very late, though less so where he was. "Everything is a mess, and I need you."

"As appealing a picture as you paint, *Mia*, I will force myself to resist getting on the next plane. Besides, I have work to do here that must be completed. Are you sick? Are you hurt?" After a moment's reflection on previous episodes in our relationship, "Are you in danger?"

"Not exactly," I sulked. I mean, it's not me exactly. There's the whole Christmas Eve dinner with the boyfriend thing, and Martha Stewart, I'm not. When did Emma turn into a traditional girlfriend type, anyway? Her attitude has always been, 'This is me, and you can take it or leave it.' This guy really has her under his thumb, and it's so unsettling. Then there's the little matter of the wedding that's taking place in our house two days after

Christmas, whether either one of is here or not. I swear, if it were for anybody besides Jeff and Donna, I'd tell them to go rent the VFW hall. And now, just when I think I've got the UCC fundraiser safely behind me, the CFO disappears in the middle of it, Santa suit and all. Where can James O'Halloran possibly be, do you suppose? I just know I'm going to get sucked into that somehow. I need you here to be on my side."

"I am always on your side, you know that, but I have never known a time when you were not either sick or hurt when you needed anyone's help. In fact, it is usually you who does the helping. This is very strange. A week ago you were looking forward to being, how do you call it, the merry widow."

"I can't be a widow without being married," I pointed out crankily.

"Whose fault is that, may I ask? Whenever we discuss it, you say, 'Soon,' or 'There's no hurry.' Is your thinking changing on this subject?" he teased me.

"How did we get onto this topic? I called to get some love and sympathy from my hunky Latino lover, and instead, I'm getting my leg pulled," I said, changing the subject.

"I am always happy to do anything that involves your legs. Of course, it is not quite so much fun over the phone."

"Mmmm," I agreed. Armando had always openly admired my legs. "Well, I can see I'm not going to get any sympathy from you, so I may as well hang up and try to get some sleep. Do you have any better idea of when you'll be able to get back?"

"Everyone on the crew is eager to return home for Christmas. Several have small children, so it especially hard on them. We are all doing our best to finish. We will have to wait and see."

"I know," I sighed.

"*Mia*? Please try not to have the house full of paramedics and police, okay?

He may have been kidding. Then again, based on our past experiences, he may not have been.

"I can't promise."

"I was afraid of that."

Not surprisingly, I spent a restless night only to fall into a heavy slumber around dawn and wind up oversleeping. At nearly seven-thirty, poor old Jasmine woke me by standing on my chest and licking my face, desperate for her breakfast. Abandoned by her feline companion of fifteen years and her favorite person in the whole world, was she now to go hungry, as well? I sprang into the kitchen to get food for her.

By forgoing my coffee stop at the diner, I managed to arrive at the UCC offices on time and let myself in, eager to learn what had become of James O'Halloran. The reception area was strangely empty. I found Shirley with the rest of the early staff arrivals in the conference room. It was an unusually subdued group that included Lois Billard. After the long night she had put in, I was impressed that she was there at all, let alone at this hour. "So that's it," she concluded her comments to the assembled staffers. "James' car was still parked on the street outside the Avery Lobby, but Mary hasn't heard from him. We haven't heard from him. His cell phone goes right to voice mail. Mary has to wait another twelve hours or so before the police will take an official missing persons report. There's nothing we can do but get on with our work and wait for word." She shrugged helplessly.

We all straggled back to our desks and attempted to get some work done, but our hearts weren't in it. At ten minutes past nine, my telephone rang. I barely recognized Mary O'Halloran. Her voice was as raw as if she had spent the night chain smoking. On second thought, maybe she had.

"Sorry to bother you, Kate, but I'm flat out of people to call and places to look. The police have been kind, but Hartford can't do anything until they know if something happened in their jurisdiction, and Wethersfield can't even take a formal missing persons report for another several hours." Her voice broke, and she paused to collect herself. "Sister Marguerite told me once that you and your partners had helped people here in town solve one or two problems in the past. Will you help me? *Can* you help me?"

I had to give the woman credit. Physically exhausted and at the end of her emotional rope, she still managed to hold it together and get right to the point.

"Of course, I'll do whatever I can, Mary. I just don't know what that might be. My friends and I aren't licensed investigators or anything. It's just that from time to time a situation crops up in the course of our real estate work, and we've been lucky enough to find some answers for the people involved."

"God knows I could use a few answers right about now. Can we talk privately? I could drive downtown and meet you somewhere. I need to get out of this house. I'm so full of caffeine, I'm about ready to jump out of my skin."

I thought for a moment. Coming to the UCC office would be awkward for her. On the other hand, I probably shouldn't go far in case I was needed here. We could always meet in the parking lot and talk in one or the other of our cars. Then I had an idea.

"How about the Cathedral, Mary? Not upstairs in the main nave but down on the lower level where we hold our meetings sometimes. I never see anyone but the maintenance men coming and going down there.

"How do I get in?" was all she asked.

"The Cathedral is always open until two in the afternoon," I assured her. "You can go right in from Farmington Avenue and down the stairs inside, and I'll meet you there. Half an hour?"

"Thank you, Kate." The gratitude in her voice was almost palpable. "I'll see you there."

Explaining that I had a personal errand to run, I gave my cell phone number to Shirley about twenty minutes later and slipped across the parking lot to the back entrance of the Cathedral. The neighborhood food bank was open, so I was able to blend in with the others standing in line before making my way across the building to the lower church hall.

Mary was already waiting for me in one of the rear pews. Her head was bowed over hands clasped so tightly together her knuckles gleamed whitely in the dim lighting. I didn't have to wonder what she was praying for. I slid into the pew beside her, and she raised a wan face to me. Last night, I had noticed how the attractive gray highlights in her brunette hair only seemed to accentuate the youthfulness of her sparkling eyes and dewy complexion. This morning, she looked every minute of her age.

"How are you holding up?" I asked her quietly. We seemed to be alone, but one never knew.

"I'm a crazy person. Certifiable. I probably shouldn't even be driving a car, but I have to go somewhere, do something. This can't be happening, but it is. My husband of twenty-seven years is missing, and nobody can seem to do anything about it, least of all me. There must be something." Her eyes begged me for suggestions. I wished with all my heart that I had some for her.

"I think the most useful thing we can do is revisit the last few days and put together a profile of James' contacts and activities that might be useful to the police when they can open an official investigation." I was totally winging it, but Mary perked right up. At last, something practical that she could focus on.

"Okay. How far back should I go?"

I pulled my little notebook out of my purse and got

ready to write. "Today's Friday. James hasn't been seen or heard from since yesterday evening. How about two or three days before that? Did anything out of the ordinary happen? Did James have any unusual appointments or meetings that you're aware of?"

"Nothing comes to mind. It was just another work week. We got up, ate breakfast, and James went to work. He was putting in some longer-than-usual hours because of preparations for the fundraiser, but so was everyone else at the UCC. I was busy with the Christmas shopping and cookie baking and getting ready for our vacation trip. James and I don't have children, you see, or close relatives who live in this area, so if we aren't traveling to spend the holiday with one or another of them, we treat ourselves to a little trip of some kind. It's usually a cruise to someplace warm. This year, we're planning to sail out of Orlando to Nassau in the Bahamas." She faltered to a stop. "I mean, it would have been the Bahamas."

I recognized the signs and braced myself for what I knew was coming. It's the verbalizing of the dashed hopes that does it. Sure enough, poor Mary heard cold, hard reality expressed in her own words, and her misery exploded into wrenching sobs. She reached out to me blindly, and I hugged her to me as she wailed with the pent-up anguish of the past eighteen hours. I knew from experience that she would have a headache from hell when the storm passed, but the release of all that anxiety and tension would restore her somewhat to herself. At least, I hoped for her sake that it would. If I were in her place, and

Armando was inexplicably among the missing, I could not imagine how I would survive it.

As her sobs downgraded to hiccups and sniffles, Mary dragged herself upright. We both dug around in our purses and unearthed enough tissues to mop up the worst of the damage. "I'm so sorry," she began, but I waved off any apologies.

"I don't know how you kept it together as long as you did," I said honestly. "Believe me, it's better to get it all out. I lived with a teenage daughter. I know. What with one boyfriend crisis or another, we'd do one of these at least once a month."

My feeble efforts at humor produced a shaky smile. "Okay, then. That's enough of that. Where were we?"

"A few days before the gala. Christmas shopping, planning for your trip. Anything else? An unusual visitor? What about James' brother Joseph? You were telling me last night that he had turned up, and you didn't seem any too pleased about it."

"Joseph, yes, that's true. He did telephone the house yesterday morning wanting to speak urgently to James. With Joseph, it's always urgent," she sniffed, "at least from his point of view. After more than twenty years of urgent calls from Joseph, we don't rise to the bait like we used to."

"Something of a black sheep, is he? Every family seems to have one."

"Mmm, well, Joseph is ours. He and James are Irish twins, you know, siblings born less than a year apart. Joseph is the younger of the two, but he and James look so much alike, they're always being mistaken for one another. Joseph always has some can't-miss financial scheme going, and of course, it's always a disaster. Over the years we must have invested twenty thousand dollars in his tax shelters and real estate developments and dot com businesses, and they fail every time. Since Joseph never contacts us unless he wants money from us, I just put yesterday's call in the back of my mind. I was going to tell James about it last night, as a matter of fact, but ..."

"Did he maybe speak to James during the day yesterday, get him on the phone at the UCC office?"

"I guess it's possible," Mary said doubtfully.

"Any chance Joseph could have something to do with James' disappearance?"

"I don't see how. All he ever wants from James is money. As soon as he gets it, he goes away."

"Where does Joseph live?"

"Somewhere in California, the last we knew. He moves around a lot. What with one failed hustle or another, he usually has a lot of people mad at him, and I know for a fact that he's stiffed more than one landlord for his rent."

"Sounds like a lovely fellow," I sympathized. "When was the last time you heard from Joseph before yesterday?"

Mary thought for a moment. "Not for more than a year. I'm sure of that, because I remember asking James last year around Christmas if he thought Joseph was likely to turn up and ruin the holiday."

"Do you think that might be what's going on now?"

"Because he called and wanted to see James? I don't know. I have no idea what he wanted. I just know from previous experience that it's never good news, no matter what tale he spins. That's why I was in no hurry to tell James about his call."

"So you're sure James didn't yet know about Joseph's call?"

"Not from me, so how else could he know? Unless Joseph did call James at the UCC," she answered her own question.

"That's possible, I suppose, but I really have no way of knowing. I'll ask Shirley if she remembers a call for James yesterday from a man she didn't recognize." I changed direction. "How has James been feeling lately? Has he been well? The fundraiser put a lot of stress on everyone, and I know there's a lot of extra reporting and paperwork that goes along with the end of the fiscal year in any organization."

"The fiscal year for most businesses coincides with the calendar year, but that's not the case with the UCC," Mary corrected me. "Their fiscal year runs from July first through June thirtieth, so that isn't an issue right now. James has been putting in quite a bit of overtime, though, because they're so short of staff. Having to lay off all those employees was just terrible for him." She grimaced.

"What layoffs? Sister Marguerite didn't mention anything about having to let people go." I didn't even try to conceal my surprise.

"About a month ago," Mary confirmed. "Nearly sixty

people were laid off from facilities all over the state, more than ten percent of the employee base."

I was astounded. "The UCC employs six hundred people? I had no idea."

Mary smiled sadly. "Very few people realize the scope of the organization or the complexity of its programs. Some of the funding comes from the member churches, but most of it comes in the form of grants from State agencies and private foundations. When those funds dry up, as they did during this recession, the staff positions they support are lost, too. James and Sister did what they could to move people into other slots, but there was only so much they could do." She shrugged.

I chewed on this for a while. "Was there anyone who took the news especially badly? You know, went ballistic?"

She shook her head slowly. "Not that I was aware of. In fact, James said that most people took the news pretty philosophically. It's more or less a fact of life in the charity business that your job depends on continued funding for the program in which you work. As bad as this economy is, most folks weren't even surprised when they got the official word, let alone devastated."

I supposed that could be true. Margo, Strutter and I had seen disaster coming months before the bottom fell out of the stock market and had retrenched accordingly to wait it out. I looked Mary full in the eyes.

"What do you think is going on here?" I asked her. "What's your gut feeling?"

Her eyes were bleak. "I haven't the first idea.

Yesterday morning, James was looking forward to playing Santa at the gala, and I was preparing for a cruise. This morning, you and I are sitting here trying to figure out what's happened to my missing husband." She turned her palms up and gazed unseeingly over my shoulder at the stained glass windows. "I just know that whatever it is, it must be very terrible for James to leave me like this."

Shortly after four-thirty, I stood for a moment in the parking lot, enjoying the crisp December air on my face. Behind me, the Cathedral parking lot was already filling with parents and children for some holiday festivity or other, and across the street the Congregational Church lot was similarly busy. I envied the churchgoers the joy they obviously found in this holiday. If I were a praying woman, this week would certainly have dropped me to my knees. That not being the case, however, I reached out to someone I knew I could count on for comfort and solace. I called Margo and smiled when she answered immediately.

"I thought you'd never get around to callin'. What's the latest on your runaway Santa? Oh, damn. Sorry, Sugar, but I've got a twelve-year-old cop with a bug up who's flashin' his lights at me. I'll have to pull over here for a sec."

"Oh, no! Where are you? What did you do?"

"God only knows, somewhere in Newington. I just fought my way out of Hartford with about three thousand commuters who were swervin' all over the place, cuttin' me off, and chattin' on the cell phones they were holding to their ears with complete impunity. Since I drive like a little old lady by comparison, I guess I'm the only one this youngster could catch. Give me a second."

There was a pause during which Margo presumably pulled over to the curb and prepared to charm the uniform pants off the young traffic cop approaching her car. A conversation between the two ensued, which was punctuated by Margo's flirtatious cooing and giggling. I strained to hear but couldn't make out the words. Perhaps two minutes passed. Margo came back on the line.

"Sorry about that. Where were we?"

"Never mind about that. How much is the ticket?"

Margo chuckled. "As if."

"You mean, you beat the rap? I hardly dare ask how."

"Oh, please. These poor guys have people mad at them all day. Our non-hostile conversation probably was a pure relief. Anyway, I'm shocked at your suggestion. You know I'm an entirely respectable married woman these days. I have to behave more appropriately than I did in my single days. Besides," she giggled again, "he was just too young, Sugar. I had to throw him back. It was the right thing to do."

I laughed with her as I imagined what putty the young officer had been in Margo's hands. In her day, she had charmed more than a few officers of the law, her husband of the last year among them. "So now that you have escaped doing hard time, can I tell you my troubles, please?"

"You bet, Hon. Tell Mother."

I proceeded to do so, complete with the details and nuances one saved for one's best friends, and was rewarded with the horrified gasps and sympathetic chuckles that I so desperately needed. "So now what do I do?" I wailed in closing, confident that help was at hand. Despite her Southern Belle persona, Margo was the most level-headed person I had ever met. Through three years of personal and professional crises, not to mention a couple of murder investigations that would bring a lesser woman to her knees, I had never seen Margo anything but poised and competent.

She considered for a moment. "Well, Sugar, for openers, I think you'd better let Strutter cook that goose for you. She'll already be makin' dinner for that huge family of hers, so one goose more or less won't even faze her. And considerin' that you're doin' the whole Norman Rockwell bit for the benefit of Emma's young man, I should think she'd be more than willin' to help you out with the weddin'. That should free you up to hold Mary O'Halloran's hand. It's not John's jurisdiction, as head of homicide, but he can find out what's goin' on with the missin' persons investigation once it gets under way. I'll have him get in touch."

Her unhesitating advice led me to marvel, not for the first time, at her efficiency. The woman was a force of nature. Probably due to my weakened state, tears filled my eyes, and I began to sniffle. "Thank you," I managed to choke as I rifled through my purse for a tissue. "You and Strutter have already done so much. It's just that Armando is away, and Mary needs my support right now, and Jasmine is so sad without Simon."

"Pish tosh," she cut my gratitude short. "Everyone will be glad to help out. It's Christmas, after all, and what are friends for? At least this time, you aren't draggin' us into a murder investigation."

 **Five**

By Saturday morning, I was in the worst mood I could remember for quite some time. Nevertheless, it was the one day I had available to accomplish the many errands that had piled up during the work week, so I dragged myself into jeans and a jacket and sallied forth. By eight o'clock, I was fighting shopping cart gridlock at the Rocky Hill Stop 'n' Shop, and after quick stops at the gas station and drugstore, I hurried home to collect Jasmine for her ten o'clock appointment with Dr. DuPont at Catzablanca, our cat clinic. Jasmine had all but stopped eating, and I was at my wits' end.

The young women at the front desk made their usual fuss over my old girl, but she didn't break into her customary purr. "What's wrong with her?" I pleaded with Dr. Linda after she had given Jasmine a thorough going over. Linda had been our trusted veterinarian for nearly twenty years. She had pulled Jasmine back from the brink of death several years back. If anyone could put her right, it was Linda. Now she took her stethoscope out of her ears and looked thoughtful as she scritched Jasmine under the chin.

"She's lonely," she finally pronounced. "Jasmine has never been an only cat. She's always been one of a herd, or at least she's had one feline companion. She's a feisty old cat, and she had her issues with Simon and Oliver and Lucy and who else came before that?"

I smiled sadly. It was true that Jasmine had outlived a number of former housemates.

"I'm just not ready for a new cat. Simon was my special boy, my loving shadow, for fifteen years. He slept with me every night and woke me up every morning. I'm still mourning him. Besides, I thought Jasmine might enjoy having the place to herself for a while."

"Obviously, she doesn't," Linda pointed out briskly. "There's nothing wrong with her physically, aside from being nearly twenty years old, but she's clearly pining. I have a kennel full of cats and kittens in the back who need good homes. Shall we go take a look?"

I knew she was right, but with everything else I had on my plate, today was not the day to adopt a new cat.

"The week after next," I promised Linda and Jasmine. "We'll do it right after Christmas. I just have to get through the holiday first."

Ten minutes later, I dumped Jasmine out of her carrier on the floor of my kitchen. As usual, she ran for the safety of the bedroom. I put a dollop of chicken baby food into her dish in case she got hungry later, then headed back to the car for my second round of errands.

The next stop was the bank, where the flu had

decimated the employee ranks. Only two tellers were open, and the line stretched out the door. I don't wait well when I'm in the best of moods, and today didn't qualify. By the time I finally made it to the head of the line, the teller and I matched each other snarl for snarl. *Ho ho ho.*

In that gloomy state of mind, I idled at the end of the bank's driveway, waiting for an opportunity to make a left onto Old Main Street. None presented itself, but what did I expect on the Saturday before Christmas? The charming shops and eating establishments of the historic district made attractive destinations for locals and tourists alike, not to mention the always popular museums. At this time of year, the exterior lights and decorations alone were sufficient to draw crowds. I was glad for the shopkeepers who were struggling in this economy but not for those of us who had to negotiate the resulting traffic.

A large Hart Seed truck lumbered by en route to its home base a mile or so down Old Main Street. I darted into the space right behind it. Almost immediately, the truck driver jammed on his brakes, and I practically had to stand on mine. "What the?" I said out loud, and then I saw what.

The truck's hazard lights began flashing, and the burly, middle-aged driver leaped out of his cab. His eyes were fixed on a pair of geese, still slim with youth. They hesitated on the far side of the road, which they clearly intended to cross. Recklessly, the driver ran to stand between them and the traffic coming out of Old Wethersfield. Time seemed to stop as I held my breath.

Traffic stopped for crossing waterfowl was a common

occurrence during the warm months of the year. Extended marshland ran about a block behind and parallel to the Silas Deane Highway, and residents were accustomed to keeping a sharp eye out for the ducks, geese and swans that unaccountably felt compelled to risk their lives to cross the roads. At this time of year, though, we expected the birds to have moved south for the winter.

After long seconds of silent consideration, the pair reached a goosey consensus and made their way across the pavement. They crossed from my left to my right and disappeared in front of the truck. The crossing safely accomplished, the driver waved briefly to acknowledge the stopped drivers and clambered back into his cab. We all went about our business.

I found myself grinning, my former pique dispersed. It had been such a small incident, but it encompassed all of the compassion and decency necessary to restore my good humor. The truck driver had stopped. Nobody had honked or screamed obscenities at him. The geese were safe in the marsh. As far as I was concerned, it was Christmas in a nutshell.

I trailed after the truck through the heart of Old Wethersfield. Without consciously intending to, I followed when it turned right into the Hart Seed Company driveway and wallowed down to the loading dock. I pulled up next to the cab and put down my window. The driver also put down his window, no doubt expecting a request for directions. "Ma'am?" he prompted.

"I just wanted you to know that was a very decent

thing you did for those geese," I said.

He looked puzzled for a moment, then, "Oh! Well, sure. I mean, I couldn't just plow over them." His seamed, weathered face reddened.

"My son is probably the only other trucker I know who would stop for an animal crossing the road."

"Oh, there's a few of us, Ma'am," the driver assured me, breaking into a bashful smile.

"Anyway, Merry Christmas," I said and put my window back up. I gave him a little wave as I headed back out the driveway. I noticed he was still smiling.

I put my deep misgivings about James O'Halloran firmly in the back of my mind and returned home with a lighter heart. I had done what I could to help Mary cope, I reminded myself, and John Harkness would keep her informed. It was time I left these relative strangers to sort out their problems for themselves and stayed focused on my own.

I usually dreaded the early dusk at this time of year. By four o'clock, the light was fading, and by five, night had fallen in earnest. The number of hours of daylight we gained or lost between the summer and winter solstices never failed to amaze me. At the end of June, each twenty-four-hour cycle included nearly sixteen hours of daylight, but by Christmas, we were lucky to have nine. The good news was that by then, the shortest day had passed, and we were once again on the upswing.

I had recruited Emma to help me decorate, and

together we spent the afternoon toiling like crazed elves. We rooted through every box in the basement and considered every garland and wreath. We even managed to drag the Christmas tree up the stairs, a task I had delegated to Armando in past years.

When the sky began to darken, I welcomed the evening as a backdrop to our handiwork. The tree stood in its corner by the door that led out to the back deck. It glittered with tiny white lights and hundreds of delicate red globes, which were generously interspersed with Joey's and Emma's favorite ornaments collected through the years. Crystal icicles competed for pride of place with an assortment of childish mementoes, most bearing a chip or a tear. In my opinion, it was perfect.

A gorgeous wreath with a fresh red ribbon adorned the front door, and a second graced the big windows in the living room. A miniature sleigh heaped with holly and pine cones made a cheerful centerpiece on the dining room table. Garland softened the mantle, which bore clusters of gleaming, scented candles, and firewood waited neatly below on the hearth. Harry Connick, Jr., crooned in the background about chestnuts roasting and Old Saint Nick. *Norman Rockwell, eat your heart out.*

Emma and I sat side by side on the sofa, Jasmine curled between us, admiring the holiday ambience we had created. A pleasant lassitude had overtaken us, assisted by the excellent Riesling we were enjoying.

"Not bad at all, if I do say so myself," Emma declared. She clinked her glass against mine.

"Glad you approve. So tell me again about this Jared we're knocking ourselves out to impress."

"Oh, it's not that bad, is it?" Emma dodged my question. "You would have decorated anyway, at least a little bit, and I always come over and help you guys put up the tree."

"That you do, Dearie." I patted her cheek. "If Joey lived closer, I'd throw myself on his mercy, but now I have Armando. Well, usually I have Armando," I amended.

"Yeah, men have a way of disappearing at the most inconvenient moments," Emma muttered to herself, and I looked at her sharply. Before I could comment, she jumped to her feet. "What do you say we give Jasmine a treat and light this gorgeous fire?'

She busied herself with the fire screen and matches. I watched fondly while she restacked the logs in the fireplace to her satisfaction and set them ablaze. Clearly, she had changed the subject, and I knew better than to pursue the topic of Jared. When your children become adults, the most important thing you can do as a mother is learn to keep your mouth shut.

Not for the first time, I marveled at the genetic quirks that had produced two such different individuals as my son and daughter from the same gene pool. Each was a unique amalgamation of Michael's and my physical traits. Emma was a slightly shorter, sturdier version of me at the same age. Her hair was my precise shade of ash blonde, though she wore hers long and loose. Her light brown eyes, flecked with green, were mine exactly, but her other features and smile were all Michael.

Joey, on the other hand, was divided neatly in two, wearing my face on his father's torso. For a year now, he had been living in Massachusetts with his girlfriend Justine. I was happy for them, but I missed seeing him as often as I had been accustomed to doing.

There had been some stormy years, but I was happy to be able to say now that I not only loved my children, I liked them.

Emma and I finished our wine and chatted companionably while Jasmine dozed on her pillow before the fireplace. When her cell phone rang, Emma leaped to retrieve it from her purse in the kitchen. Two minutes later, she was out the door.

"He's a jerk," said Joey later that evening. He had telephoned as I was trying to decide which of the unappealing leftovers in the refrigerator would constitute my dinner. "He teaches math at some expensive sports academy in Bangor. He won some minor medal in a regional competition a few years back, so the New England Sports Institute hired him." Joey's disgust was evident, but I wasn't getting any information from Emma, so I pressed on.

"The New England Sports Institute is ...?" I opened the lid of a plastic container and sniffed cautiously. Beef stew, I was pretty sure. How had I so completely lost the knack of cooking for just one person?

"It's a private school for the sons of the ridiculously rich and once famous. If your kid can't get out of the tenth grade, and you can afford the outrageous tuition, the Institute will grease his way through the academics and teach him more than anybody needs to know about Foosball."

"Now you're really lost me. What's that?" I replaced the lid on the container and put it back in the refrigerator. *Chinese take-out it is. Again.*

"I don't know either. I just like the word. Bogey, get off the counter!"

I smiled as I imagined Joey's big, amiable tabby cat oozing guiltily off the forbidden surface.

"So Jared is in Maine most of the time, but Emma is so smitten that she hangs around waiting for his nightly telephone call. Is that what you're telling me?"

"Yep, except I doubt that it's nightly."

"This doesn't sound at all like your sister. Emma has burned through a couple of dozen boyfriends since high school, but I can't remember her playing this part. Oh, there were one or two who got to her when she was a teenager, but since then, she's always been the one who plays hard to get. If Mr. Wonderful of the Moment doesn't make the grade, he's shown the door. What's the major attraction, do you suppose?"

A rumbling purr reached my ear while Joey thought about it. I assumed that Bogey had been forgiven and was now in Joey's lap.

"Beats me, Ma. He's really good looking, for one thing."

"*Really* good looking," put in Justine from the background. Joey snorted.

"See what I mean? And he's got the sports star thing going for him."

"How did they even meet?"

"His parents live in West Hartford. They met when he was in Connecticut visiting them a couple of months ago. He looked up Emma the next time he was down there for the weekend, and she visited him in Maine once. I think she fell in love with the whole New England prep school mystique. She sees herself living on this picture-perfect campus surrounded by a bunch of rowdy kids who adore her and call her ma'am or something."

I could see how that might appeal to Emma. Her heart had always gone out to kids.

"Or maybe it's just sex," Joey mused.

"Joey!" Justine and I protested simultaneously. "Please remember you're talking to your mother here," I begged. "Well, this promises to be an interesting Christmas Eve. I don't even know if Armando will make it home in time. How do you and Justine feel about roast goose?"

"Yuck."

Perfect.

Late Sunday morning, I met Strutter and Margo at the Town Line Diner for brunch. We had agreed that what used to be an occasional indulgence would become a regular date as we waited out the slump in the real estate market. We caught up on the few clients who were new to us and shared information on Vista Views, the retirement community that kept us on retainer in the wild hope that one of these days, we would sell a unit. Then we moved on to more interesting topics like family and food and men.

This morning, we shelved that last topic, since Margo's husband John was with us. The handsome Lieutenant Harkness was in charge of homicide and other major investigations for the Wethersfield Police Department. Our paths had crossed as a result of two situations in which we had been involved during the past two years, totally involuntarily. "The homicide biz certainly has picked up since the three of you came to town," John had been heard to comment a bit sarcastically. Watching how Old Hardnose, as he was called by his subordinates, blossomed under Margo's adoring attentions, I didn't think he had any serious complaints. The man practically purred with contentment.

"I don't know how you gals do this every week and keep your figures," he said now, patting his midsection. "Another one of those omelets, and I won't be able to buckle my belt."

"It's all a part of my master plan, Darlin'. You know I'll do whatever it takes to get those trousers off you." Margo winked at him across her coffee cup, and John blushed to the roots of his hair. After a year of marriage, he still squirmed uncomfortably at Margo's lascivious repartee.

"Is there anywhere in the world you can go these days to escape people yapping on their cell phones?" Strutter helped him out by changing the subject as a particularly obnoxious ringtone sounded in the booth across the aisle from us. The matron to whom it belonged dug furiously in her purse for several seconds and finally produced the thing.

"HELLO, PHYLLIS? YES, I CAN HEAR YOU NOW. CAN YOU HEAR ME?" she yelled into it. We all cringed.

"Well, we can sure as hell hear you, as can most of the people sittin' in this restaurant tryin' to enjoy their breakfasts," Margo sighed.

"I'M HAVING BREAKFAST WITH GINNIE AT THE DINER BEFORE WE GET ON THE ROAD. NO, THE DINER, THE DINER! D-I-N-E-R. YOU KNOW, THE ONE AT EXIT 24 OFF THE HIGHWAY WHERE WE HAD LUNCH THAT TIME YOU AND HARRY VISITED. THE COFFEE WAS SO GOOD THAT HARRY DRANK TOO MUCH, AND YOU HAD TO STOP THREE TIMES ON THE WAY HOME SO HE COULD PEE." She brayed with laughter at her naughty story and started to cough. Her companion looked embarrassed and slapped her on the back rather harder than was necessary, I noted.

"Why do they always have to yell?" I wondered aloud. "If Phyllis was here at the diner with her, she'd speak to her in a normal tone of voice, but you hand someone a cell phone, and the volume triples." I glared at the offender across the aisle. "It's very annoying."

John had been silent, but now he chimed in. "I've noticed that a lot of places have started putting signs up at the entrance asking patrons to turn off their cell phones while they're inside. I think it's a good idea. Why don't you suggest it to the owners here? The three of you eat here all the time. I'm sure they wouldn't mind a constructive comment."

"I'll do it on the way out today," I promised.

Two cell phones rang simultaneously in our booth. Strutter rolled her eyes as John and I looked at each other in embarrassment. He began slapping his pockets, and I fumbled for my purse beneath the table. Margo snorted into her coffee cup, that inelegant response she had when something struck her as amusing. John slid out of the booth and headed for the exit, his phone to his ear, while I slapped at Strutter's legs underneath the table. She cackled with glee as I struggled to retrieve my purse.

"It's your fault," I hissed. "I never have the damned thing on except when we're supposed to meet somewhere."

"Read my lips," she responded serenely. "Vibrate."

I snatched the offending device out of my purse and flipped it open. "If this is a telemarketer, boy, did you get a wrong number."

I was horrified to hear Mary O'Halloran's voice, which trembled with tears. Her obvious agony stabbed me to the heart. "I'm so sorry. I didn't know who else to call. It's been more than forty-eight hours now, and the police haven't come up with a single lead."

I flapped a hand at Margo and Strutter to stop their giggling. "Mary O'Halloran," I mouthed silently.

"It's fine, Mary. I was just being stupid. Did you tell the police all the things you and I talked about on Friday? What about Joseph? Have they been able to locate him?"

"Oh, God, I talked to them for hours and hours," Mary moaned. "They know as much as I do about James' family, friends, educational background, hobbies, old girlfriends, bank accounts, everything. They wanted to know if he's addicted to anything, Kate, or if I think he might be cheating on me. *Cheating* on me." She blew her nose. "As for Joseph, it's as if he never existed. He hasn't been at the last address we have for him in California for more than a year, and the cell phone number he gave me goes right to voice mail. I'm at the end of my rope, Kate."

John returned to the table looking somber. He motioned to me to hang up.

"Mary, listen. I have to go right now, but I'll call you back in just a few minutes, okay? I'm sure we'll know more very soon. Hang in there just a little longer."

"Kate?" It was as if Mary, too, sensed that important information was about to be forthcoming. "If you learn anything, anything at all, please tell me. It's been long enough now that the news probably won't be good, but I can take it. Anything is better than this not knowing. Promise me."

I assessed John's grim expression before answering her, but she had a point. Not knowing had to be the absolute worst.

"I promise," I assured her and ended the call. Across the aisle, Ginnie and her companion stared curiously. John eased his lanky frame back into the booth beside Margo and turned his back on them. He spoke quietly.

"A body just washed up in Wethersfield Cove."

"James O'Halloran?" I blurted, wanting him to deny it.

"The odds are good, I'm afraid. It's a middle-aged man wearing a Santa Claus suit."

Six

"What's the address?" Margo asked, and I realized that I didn't know.

"I'll drive. I sold them their house, remember." Strutter led the way to her gray Lexus, a dignified vehicle that seemed to fit the circumstances.

I had relayed to Mary as gently as possible what John had told me about James' body washing up in the Cove. I explained that the coroner would be asking her to come in and identify the remains at some point and offered to accompany her.

"Oh, please, please!" she begged in a ragged voice. "Let me see him now. I can't sit here waiting for an official call. If you won't come and get me, I'm going to drive myself to the Cove this minute. There has to be an end to this."

"Not a good idea," John pronounced. "No telling what condition the body is in after days in the water. At least let the coroner's crew get him cleaned up a little before she has to view the remains."

"If we don't bring her, John, she'll drive herself. She knows where he is."

John shot Margo a "Help me!" look.

"It will be terrible for Mary wherever she has to do this, Darlin'," she reminded him softly. "The images are already in her mind. At least this way, she won't have to drive herself, and we'll be there to support her."

He gave up. "It's a public place. If she shows up against my advice, there's nothing I can do about it."

"Will the police at the scene allow her to see him?" Strutter put in.

"They will if John tells them to. In any event, they won't be able to stop her," I predicted, "even if she has to climb over the crime scene tape and take down a couple of officers to do it."

Mary was waiting for us at the door of the cozy, gray-shingled Cape Cod house on Wolcott Hill Road. She wore slacks and a sweater in decorous gray and a camelhair coat. Her make-up was subdued but in place. She accepted the front passenger seat, and Margo joined me in the back.

"Thank you for doing this, all of you," she offered in a voice that was perfectly composed.

Strutter looked at us in the rearview mirror. *This woman is on the ragged edge,* she telegraphed before putting the Lexus into reverse, as if we had any doubts. We were all silent on the short trip. Wethersfield Cove is a natural inlet on the Connecticut River. It lies on the far side of the historic district where Old Main Street runs out at the bottom of a long grade. The parking lot extends all the way to the water's edge.

A recent rain had swelled the river and raised the water level in the Cove. Two police cruisers, a black sedan, and an ambulance were clustered near a small knot of official personnel at the water's edge that included John Harkness. Strutter pulled up next to the black sedan, and we all got out. John spoke briefly to one of the young officers and came to join us.

Mary's composure was becoming downright eerie. "May I please see my husband, Lieutenant?"

"It's not too bad," John said to us all, but mostly to Mary. "The water is cold at this time of year, so ..." he didn't finish. He didn't have to.

The men at the scene had obviously been forewarned of Mary's arrival and had done what they could to soften the appearance of the body without interfering with the work of the coroner. James lay face down in the sand in his sodden, garish Santa Claus garb. His head was turned to the left, the skin blue and the lips pale. His left hand was raised above his head. A blanket covered most of his torso, which must have been grotesquely bloated.

Mary approached the little tableau calmly with Margo and me on either side of her. Strutter brought up the rear, averting her eyes. The men stepped aside, their faces displaying professional sympathy, and allowed us to stand only a few feet from the remains. For a few seconds, Mary gazed almost tenderly at the body before us. Then she stiffened. Margo and I each grabbed an arm, not knowing what to expect.

"It's not James," Mary said finally. "Oh my God, it's not my husband." With that, she dropped to her knees in the sand and collapsed into tears.

Strutter, the natural mother of our group, knelt beside Mary to comfort her. Margo and I reluctantly stepped closer to the body for a better look.

"That's James," I told her and John. "His glasses are gone, but I saw him several times before Thursday night. I sat across from him at a meeting, and that's him. Look, there's his bald spot. I remember seeing it when I was behind him in the crowd Thursday night. He was on his way to the Education Office to change into the very suit he's wearing now. Poor Mary," I finished up. "She simply can't face the truth."

"Who can blame her?" said Margo, hugging John's arm. "I'd be in complete denial, too."

"No!" Mary wailed. "No, no, no!" She broke free of Strutter's restraining arms and scrambled to her feet. "He's not wearing a wedding ring. James hasn't taken off his wedding band since the day we were married."

"I'm sorry, Ma'am, but that could have happened in the water," said one of the young officers apologetically.

Mary dragged the sleeve of her coat across her streaming eyes and nose and shook her finger at the bloated corpse. "You're not listening to me, Officer. Do you really believe that a wife of more than thirty years wouldn't recognize her husband? That man has a bald spot on the back of his head. My husband had a full head of hair. That body is not James O'Halloran. It's his brother Joseph."

The mood at the UCC on Monday morning was somber. The easy banter among collegial staff members had been replaced with uncertain courtesy. News of the discovery of Joseph's body, along with James' inexplicable disappearance, had spread through the ranks like wildfire. Everyone was fairly bursting with questions for which there were no answers.

Far from achieving closure, Mary O'Halloran had had hysterics at the edge of the Cove. A second ambulance had been summoned to transport her to Hartford Hospital, where she had been admitted overnight for observation. A concerned neighbor woman knocked on the O'Hallorans' door while Strutter was packing a bag for Mary. She offered to lock up the house and even to stay with Mary when she was released, which relieved us all mightily.

" 'Tis a sad turn of events to be sure," Sister Marguerite said for the fourth time that morning. On this occasion, it was to the Archbishop of the Hartford diocese with whom she was talking on the phone. "I will certainly keep you informed. Thank you for calling." She hung up and sighed. "The problem is that we have no information to share. This thing is a complete mystery."

Aloysius, snug in his corner bed, thumped his tail in agreement. Since I had no comfort or insights to offer, I took myself back to my desk to be of what practical assistance I could manage.

Before I tackled the welter of post-gala paperwork that awaited me, I went in search of a much-needed cup of coffee, which my nose told me Shirley had just brewed. I met up with her in the little kitchenette.

"Good morning, Kate," was her unusually subdued greeting. She absently straightened one of the many little Christmas trees that fairly littered the place. Last week, they had struck me as whimsical and festive. This morning, they clashed sourly with the mood of the people who worked in the building. "I wonder if I should put all this stuff back in the basement," Shirley read my thoughts.

"I wouldn't," I said, pouring out my coffee. "The clients and others who come through here would find it odd, don't you think?"

"I guess." She looked around uncertainly. "It just feels inappropriate somehow, like wearing a red dress to a funeral."

Her analogy made me smile. "Shirley, can you think back to Thursday before everyone left to go over to the Wadsworth?" I followed her back to her desk in the reception area. "Do you remember if anyone called James that day whose voice you didn't recognize? A man, middle aged. Probably didn't want to give you his name."

"You mean the brother, don't you? The one whose body was found yesterday." She shuddered. "I've been up all night thinking about him. Why didn't we know anything about this brother. Joseph, is it?"

I nodded. "He was a bit of a black sheep, according to James' wife. Turned up every few years when he needed money for one of his crazy financial schemes. He was in the area that day, because he called the house, and I believe I saw him at the gala Thursday night. He looked so much like his brother, I mistook him for James. What we can't figure out is how he got into the Wadsworth to begin with."

"It wouldn't have been that difficult, considering all of the volunteers we had to recruit at the last minute to replace the people who were down with the flu," Shirley reminded me. She had a good point. There was a semi-official list started by Mary Alice before she was ordered home to bed, but over the last couple of weeks, that had pretty much deteriorated. I myself had recruited Strutter and Margo to help out. I didn't even remember if I gave their names to Lois Billard or Shirley or anyone else who might have been interested. By Thursday afternoon, we had just been grateful when the majority of our eleventh-hour volunteers actually showed up.

"To answer your question, no, I don't remember a call to James from a man. There was a woman, though." She squeezed her eyes shut. "Yes, I'm fairly certain that was on Thursday. It had to be, because James wasn't here after that."

I was surprised by this unexpected curve. "A woman called James here? How old a woman? Did she have an accent of any kind? Sorry," I apologized. "It's just the first possible lead we've had since James disappeared. Can you remember anything at all?"

She thought for a moment. "It was fairly early. I had just taken the phone off the night system, and it rang immediately. I remember, because I was making the coffee, and it interrupted me."

I knew how much Shirley relished her morning coffee and could well imagine her annoyance.

"What did she say?" I prompted.

"She asked specifically for James, but there was something odd about the way she did it, as if she didn't really know him."

"Did she ask for Mr. O'Halloran? Or maybe she got his name a little wrong?"

"That's it. She called him Jim. I've never known anyone to call him Jim or Jimmy, so at first I thought it was a telemarketer, one of those brash ones that try to get by you by acting too familiar."

"Jim, hmmm. Then what?"

"Well, I told her he wasn't in the office yet and put her through to his voice mailbox. When James came in a few minutes later, I told him he had a message waiting, and that was that."

"No other calls?"

She stirred her coffee and tried to remember. "I don't think so, Kate, but the place was a madhouse that morning. We were all running around trying to get ready to go over to the Wadsworth. I wasn't the only one answering the phone. When it rang, whoever was nearest picked it up. You know how it can get."

I did indeed know how it could get. The office would never qualify as spacious, even for the twenty or so employees who worked there. Add delivery people, clients, and other visitors coming in for meetings or what have you, and things could be very crowded and noisy. By contrast, the place seemed unnaturally quiet today.

When I returned to my desk, the message light on the phone was blinking. "I'm working at home today, Kate," said the IT Coordinator in my ear. Marilyn was a vivacious redhead whose staggering task it was to keep all of the UCC's employees networked. "Do me a favor and change the back-up tape in the server, would you?'

I was happy to help Marilyn out, of course, but technical expertise has never been my strong point. I was a little nonplussed, but if Marilyn thought I could handle it, I reasoned, then I probably could. She would never expose the computer equipment to possible damage by the technically inept.

Following her instructions, I collected one of the numbered cassettes and the keys to the server cage from her office, then headed up the stairs to the second floor of the building. Only a few cubicles were occupied, and all of the half-dozen offices belonging to the senior managers were dark. I looked around uncertainly for the staircase leading to the unfinished third floor, where Marilyn had said the server was located.

"Changing the tape?" asked a cheerful youngster from behind a pile of cardboard-bound grants and proposals on her desk. I recognized her as the development director's assistant but couldn't quite come up with her name. "We all have to do that once in a while. Stairs are back there. Just feel for the light switch when you open the door." She pointed over her shoulder to the unmarked door at the end of the short aisle.

I smiled my thanks and went on my way. The plain, white door was unlocked. I twisted the knob and saw the shape of stairs on my left. Stepping in, I felt along the wall and located a switch. Fumbling a little with my hands full, I finally managed to flip it and was relieved when bright light illuminated a wide, wooden staircase. The prospect of visiting the attic of this old house wouldn't have thrilled me under the most benign of circumstances, and the events of the last few days had been unsettling.

A scurrying sound stopped me in my tracks. Had it been real or imaginary? The residents and workers of Asylum Hill might know this was now the administrative office of the United Christian Coalition, but did the squirrels and other rodents? I held my breath but heard nothing further. *Oh, just get it over with,* I scolded myself and stamped up the stairs, jangling the keys to encourage any furry residents to retreat to their lairs.

The server housing at the top of the stairs was modern and well lit, and the key turned smoothly in the lock. Changing the tape took only a few seconds. I was soon relocking the cage from the outside. The stacked electronic gizmos hummed reassuringly.

Having accomplished my task without destroying anything, I felt brave enough to take a quick look around before returning to the first floor. The wintry sunlight streaming through several small windows cheered the big space, which was surprisingly uncluttered. I had anticipated piles of archived files and jangly piles of discarded office paraphernalia, but only one stack of large cartons occupied a far corner. The boxes were draped with a tarpaulin, leading me to believe that the roof might have a leak or two.

In my short time at the UCC, I had learned that social workers tended to be packrats. Their workspaces were filled with papers, books and files organized in ways understandable only to themselves. Up here, though, I could imagine what the old house had been like originally. I could easily picture Jo Marsh of *Little Women* curled up on an old sofa by that window over there, eating apples and scribbling her stories.

Another round of furtive rustling snapped me out of my reverie, and I hurried back down the stairs to the paperwork that awaited me.

"Jasmine would have loved it," I told Margo on the phone that evening as I sat with the old cat on the living room sofa. She lapped uninterestedly at the chicken baby food with which I was trying to tempt her appetite. "Lots of hidey holes for mice and squirrels and who knows what else. Probably a few bats under the eaves, too. She would have had a grand old time."

"How are things comin' along with the weddin'?" Margo asked, more to change the subject than out of any burning interest, I suspected. My friends were tiring of the drama at the UCC, and who could blame them? I was growing weary of it myself.

"Fine, I guess. Emma contacted the maid of honor, and she seems to have things pretty well in hand. I emailed Michael from work today to ask if there's anything special I should be doing. He said not to worry. Jeff and Donna are very excited about having a small wedding among family, and the caterer has everything handled."

"That must be some caterer. Everything is all set, but he's never even seen your place?" Margo said doubtfully.

"Michael gave him a floor plan, which is how a lot of these smaller events are worked out in advance. I guess they draft a preliminary layout for the seating and food, get menu approval, then finalize the schedule and the staffing. Much more efficient than sending actual people out to inspect every location personally. Michael and Sheila say it's going to be lovely." I looked around my decorated-to-the-hilt living room. "My major worry right now is Christmas Eve. Emma is so besotted with this Jared person, it worries me."

"What's the big attraction?" Margo wanted to know. Now we were in her area of expertise.

"Joey and Justine say he's a hunk, some kind of minor sports star, but Emma has dated plenty of good-looking guys before. She could always take them or leave them. This one is different."

Margo chuckled. "As you know, I like men better 'n I like chocolate candy, but I could always take or leave 'em both. That is, until my John came along. Do you think that's what's goin' on with Emma? Is this fellow the one?"

"Never having met him, it's hard for me to say. He's in Maine most of the time teaching snowboarding, of all the unlikely things, to the sons of the filthy rich. Joey doesn't think much of him. He didn't come right out and say it, but I got the impression that he suspects that Jared isn't all that into Emma."

"Oh, dear. It's always the elusive devils that get under a girl's skin. On that topic, what do you hear from your absent man?"

I filled her in on what little I knew about Armando's business trip. "If he doesn't make it back for Christmas Eve, I'll be beside myself," I finished up. "I thought I'd love every minute of my solitude, but what I wouldn't give to hear him coming in the door right about now."

"I love that sound myself," Margo sympathized. "Speakin' of which, excuse me for a sec, Sugar. John is comin' in this very minute."

She disappeared, and I listened enviously to smoochy noises and giggles as she greeted her husband. To my surprise, it was John who picked up the phone.

"Kate? John here. I've got some new information on the Santa situation."

"About James? Have you located him?"

"No, sorry. It's about the brother."

"Has the body been identified officially as Joseph O'Halloran?"

"Technically speaking, his sister-in-law's identification is sufficient, but since he died under suspicious circumstances, and his next of kin, brother James, is the subject of a missing persons investigation, we're treating this one as a probable homicide. The L.A.P.D. ran a check and came up with quite a few priors on Joseph, fraud, embezzlement and so on. All dismissed ultimately, no convictions, but that's not the real news."

I wasn't at all sure I wanted to know the real news, but John so obviously wanted to tell me, it seemed impolite not to give him the opportunity.

"What is it, John?"

"Joseph died of asphyxiation, drowning, to be exact. We figured that, even though there was a large contusion on his right temple that looked as if it could have killed him. We thought he was probably knocked unconscious and then dumped in the river, where he drowned."

"Okay. So?"

"The thing is, his lungs weren't filled with river water. They were filled with champagne punch."

 **Seven**

The last time I had visited the O'Hallorans' house, I had seen only the outside of the snug Cape. This time, I was ushered inside by Mary's neighbor. Presumably, she was the same one who had volunteered to keep an eye on Mary a few days ago, but I couldn't be sure. Neighborhoods, particularly those whose residents are long established, have intricate support systems that have evolved over the years.

"I'll be right next door if you need me," the woman called to Mary over her shoulder. "She's in the kitchen," she said to me. "I think she's stronger today." With that, she let herself out and vanished across the front lawn.

I followed the aroma of fresh coffee past the center staircase to the back of the house. As many buyers of these 1950s-era homes do, James and Mary had removed the walls between the front and back rooms to open up the downstairs. The result was a surprisingly spacious living room on the left and a cheerful, well-lit kitchen/dining room on the right.

I had rather expected to find Mary slouched in a chair, still in her bathrobe, but I was reassured to find her arranging coffee things on a tray in her tidy kitchen. She was dressed in tailored slacks and a soft sweater. Her make-up had been carefully applied, and her hair was in place, although the gray I had noticed last week seemed somehow more pronounced.

"Thanks for coming, Kate." Her smile was as warm as ever. "Shall we have our coffee in the living room? The morning sun is so cheerful in there."

I picked up the filled carafe and followed her down a short hallway to the rear of the living room. A wide window overlooking the back yard allowed the sun to warm our backs nicely as we sat on the sofa in front of it.

"You look well, Mary. How are you doing?" I took a sip of excellent coffee.

"Better," she answered sturdily. "I went to the Cove on Sunday prepared to identify my dead husband. Anything short of having to do that is solvable. That's why I wanted to see you in person, Kate. Thank you, by the way. I know you were expected at the UCC this morning. The post-fundraiser week is always a hectic one, and without James, well, I'm sure everyone is doing the best they can."

"My being here isn't a problem," I assured Mary. "Sister Marguerite and Lois and Shirley and James' assistant are all half out of their minds with concern for James and for you, as well. Solving this mystery and reuniting you is everyone's most fervent wish, so if there's any way at all that I can help, believe me when I say I'm more than happy to do it."

I took another sip of coffee, hoping I had opened the door sufficiently for Mary to tell me why she had asked me to come by this morning. Her early phone call had taken me by surprise. She put down her mug and composed her hands in her lap.

"I'm afraid I haven't been entirely forthcoming. There was another phone call last Thursday morning besides the one from Joseph." She regarded me levelly. "I didn't mention it sooner, because it's a private matter, and quite frankly, I was embarrassed. At the time, I couldn't imagine that it had anything to do with all of this. Now, I'm fairly certain it does."

I remembered what Shirley had told me about James' message from an unfamiliar female caller. "Was it from a woman?" I asked Mary now.

Her fingers twisted together in agitation, but she met my gaze. "Yes. It was from Roberta."

I searched my memory but came up empty. "I'm sorry. Who is Roberta?"

"I don't know her last name. I never have. The only thing I do know is that she and James were involved briefly some years ago. They had an affair," she concluded to clarify the nature of their involvement, which I had already guessed. It's always the quiet ones who fool you.

"You know this because …?"

"James told me." Mary smiled bleakly. "It's the downside of having an honest, committed relationship.

You're spared nothing, even the knowledge of things you'd be much happier not knowing."

She picked up the carafe and held it up questioningly. I shook my head, and she refilled her mug. I kept silent and waited.

"It was at a convention in California," she continued. "All of the top financial executives from charitable organizations all over the country meet once a year to be updated on new legislation, tax regulations, that sort of thing. The bean counters' convention, James calls it. It's a huge snore. I never went. None of the wives did." She made a face. "I probably should have, as it turns out."

"Convention fever, we called it when I worked with the management company of an international trade show. Relationships are spawned out of sheer boredom." I smiled to assure Mary that I didn't find her news shocking. It had been my experience that, given the chance, boys would be boys. So would most men.

"Yes," Mary agreed, "but there was a little more to it. James and I had had quite a serious quarrel just before he left for that particular convention. I can't even remember now what it was about." She shrugged. "Whatever it was, it was enough for James to justify to himself having his little fling with Roberta, at least for the few days they were in California. He told me that as soon as he got on the plane to come home, he was overcome with remorse. By the time he arrived here, he had worked himself into quite a state." Her face clouded over at the memory.

"He told you right away, then?"

"Immediately. He didn't even say hello, just flung open the door and blurted it all out. He looked so awful, Kate, I thought someone had died, or he had an incurable disease or something. It was almost a relief to find out it was just a stupid affair. Almost," she repeated with a trace of bitterness.

I held out my mug, ready for a refill. "Then what happened?"

"He felt better, and I felt terrible. That's how these things usually go, isn't it? I hated him for about a week. Then I forgave him."

I nodded my understanding. "Was that the end of it?"

"I thought so at the time, but about a year later, there were some phone calls. James told me they were from Roberta. He said she was ill and had lost her job, needed some money. If I didn't object, he wanted to loan her a thousand dollars. I told him I didn't object, but I never quite believed that story." She smiled to herself. "James is basically a truthful person, so he lies very badly." She was quiet for a moment, remembering.

"What do you think the true story was, or should I say, is?" I prompted her.

She sipped her coffee thoughtfully. "I believe there's a child, a boy. Again, there's nothing terribly unusual about that, except that James and I were never lucky enough to have children. So when Roberta produced a son and heir, that rather put her in the catbird seat."

I didn't follow her reasoning and said so.

"Don't you see? In James' eyes, she went from being his former fling to being the mother of his only child, which is quite an elevation in status, wouldn't you agree?"

"How do you really know all this, Mary? Did James tell you ultimately?"

She shook her head. "No. That would have been far too hurtful, to his way of thinking. The fact that Roberta had borne his child meant that it was my fault James and I had never conceived, you see. He knew that would cause me real suffering."

I tried to take this in. "Aren't you just assuming all of this? I mean, if he never told you, what makes you believe there's a child?"

Mary's eyes clouded once again, and she stirred her coffee, now cold, with ferocity. "There was a picture," she said finally, "one of those awful school photos. A small boy with slicked-back hair and a missing tooth in the front. I found it in the pocket of James' navy blue blazer after one of his convention trips several years later. The boy was the spitting image of James."

I was silent as I considered how very terrible that discovery must have been for her, to be betrayed yet again and realize that her beloved husband was apparently prepared to go on lying to her forever.

"How could you forgive him after that, Mary?"

"It does seem impossible, I know, but the first time, it was all about him, his feelings, what he wanted or thought he wanted. But after that, it was all about the child—his name is Patrick, by the way—and me. As soon as he knew there was a child, James did everything he could for Patrick. When I started missing money from our accounts, I knew where it was going. There were calls from his attorney to confirm meetings I wasn't supposed to know about but did. Now and then, he would slip up and leave a statement lying around for the trust fund he established for Patrick, things like that."

I was stunned, and my face must have shown it. "You said nothing? All these years?"

"James was trying so desperately to spare me the knowledge of Patrick while still doing right by his son. How could I let him know that he had failed?"

I couldn't help spluttering in indignation. "The money involved must have been considerable. How could James believe you wouldn't notice, Mary?"

She smiled at my perplexity. "He had to believe he was succeeding, Kate. He simply could not bear to hurt me again, not in this terrible way. So he bore his burden in silence and took what comfort he could from his belief that at least he was sparing my feelings. He loves me, Kate. Can you possibly understand that? I love him, and he loves me. Of that, I am very, very certain."

After leaving Mary, I stopped by the diner and picked up a cup of their good coffee to go. Not wanting to be one of those annoying people who yap on their cell phones in public places, I took it back out to the Jetta to sip while I shared Mary's new theory with Margo.

"Can you imagine your husband keeping a secret like that from you, and your letting him?" I finished up. "I mean, the convention fling with Roberta, maybe, but to find out six or eight years later that there's a child, and James was supporting him all that time and still keeping it a secret? I don't think so."

"Well, I suppose it's better than findin' out there's a child, and he's not supportin' him," Margo mused. "It's the secretive part that would be the most upsettin' to me. I'm still tryin' to get my head around the fact that this nice, conservative man who spends his life slavin' away for a charitable organization has a wife who's completely nuts about him, an ex-lover, an illegitimate son, a black sheep brother who turns up drowned, and, oh, yes, has now gone missin' himself. Honestly, Sugar, you couldn't make this stuff up. So now what?"

"Now I get myself to work. If Mary follows my advice, she calls your husband, and the police track down this Roberta to see what, if anything, she knows about this whole situation."

"How can they do that? All they have to go on is her first name."

"Oh, there's way more to go on than that. Someone at the UCC will know the name of the organization that sponsors the annual conventions James attends. That organization will have rosters of members and past attendees. In the universe of charity CFOs, there can't be all that many women, period, and surely not more than one or two named Roberta."

"I see your point. How's Strutter doin', by the way? Have you talked with her?"

"Not since Sunday, now that you mention it."

"Huh. Me neither. I think I'll give her a call and see what's cookin'."

"Say hi for me, and speaking of cooking, ask her what I owe her for that Christmas Eve goose she's doing for me. Gotta go."

I threaded my way through the light midmorning traffic on automatic pilot, my mind still whirling from Mary's revelations. I had no doubt that Mary was right about one thing. James loved her. I had spoken to the man only a couple of times in the days before the gala, and Mary's name had come up both times. His references to her were affectionate, even doting. So why had he jeopardized his long-time marriage to a woman he clearly adored by having a convention fling?

Mary had said they'd had a quarrel just before he left on his trip, but was that so very unusual? Armando and I weren't even married yet, and we certainly quarreled from time to time. Nothing of real consequence, mostly just a lot of hissing and spitting, but still. He also was on the road for TeleCom now and again. Was this what lay in store for me?

I pulled into the UCC parking lot and was surprised to see more cars than usual. Then I remembered the extensive post-gala meeting scheduled for ten-thirty with everyone who had anything to do with the fundraiser. The group was too large for the conference room in the UCC office, so the plan was to gather in the lower level of the Cathedral. I looked at my watch, which said ten-forty-five. Probably not too late to be noticeable, if previous meetings were any indication. Starting times were always loose.

I locked up the Jetta and sprinted for the back door at the lower level of the Cathedral. Following the hubbub of conversation, I headed down a flight of stairs and came to the large, lower nave, where the meeting was just getting under way. I smiled and nodded to one of the many maintenance staff members who kept the Cathedral in order, not sure enough of his name to risk saying it out loud. With seconds to spare, I skinned into a rear pew next to the entryway I had just passed through.

After James' assistant began his financial report, I took note of my surroundings once again. There was certainly a lot to see, since St. Joseph's was one of the largest cathedrals in Connecticut. As I had noted during our previous meeting here in the lower level, the ambience was impressive and would have been even without the Christmas decorations that now festooned every nook and cranny. The hundred or so people in attendance occupied only a small percentage of the available pews, and stained glass windows filled most of the wall opposite me. I wondered again what the main floor of the Cathedral would look like. As luck would have it, I got my chance to find out.

It seemed very cold to me, probably because I had left my coat in the car and had forgotten to bring a sweater with me. As the speaker droned on about debits and credits and balance sheets, I eased out of the pew and back to the entrance. I intended to go back to the parking lot to collect my coat, but at the bottom of the stairs, I paused. Someone upstairs was playing the pipe organ, the magnificent Mighty Austin about which I had heard.

As if drawn by a magnet, I tiptoed up to the main level to investigate and found the doors to the nave standing wide open. To my astonishment, no mass was in progress. What seemed like acres of empty pews, each and every one adorned with an evergreen swag, stood before me. I nearly gasped aloud at the grandeur of the altar, banked with row upon row of potted poinsettias. But the main draw to my senses was the organ music. Someone was playing the Austin, and without even thinking about it, in I went. I might not be a religious person, but Christmas music, impressively performed, could still produce gooseflesh. I crept inside and gazed around me.

If the stained glass windows of the lower level had been impressive, those on this level could only be described as awe-inspiring, which I supposed was the intention. The enormous pillars required to support the massive upper structure afforded me cover as I endeavored to trace the source of the music. After a few minutes of neck-craning, I was rewarded with the sight of an organist at the keyboard in the loft on the mezzanine level. Having spotted him, I withdrew once again to stand quietly behind a sheltering column, not wanting to make him self-conscious about having an unexpected audience.

I looked about at my new surroundings as the music

swelled and ebbed around me in the impeccable acoustics. "In dulci jubilo," I thought, although the name of the composer escaped me. The altar, which lay a hundred yards in front of me, was a breathtaking configuration of architectural details and sculptures. The right wall of the nave was filled with what seemed to be confessionals, if my sketchy knowledge of the Catholic faith was accurate. Cautiously, I lowered myself into a pew and closed my eyes as the organist struggled to get a particularly complicated sequence exactly right, repeating a few bars of the music over and over. When he had mastered the passage, he played it triumphantly, and the reverberation of the huge pipes that had been installed throughout the Cathedral made me shiver.

Shirley had told me that more than eight thousand pipes had been built into the walls, some so big they had been installed before the roof was completed. I hugged myself in sheer delight. Perhaps there was something left about Christmas for me to enjoy.

The sound of approaching footsteps snapped me back to reality, and I guiltily headed for the door as George, or was it Mark, entered the nave carrying a mop and bucket. "I couldn't resist," I whispered as I passed him, and he grinned conspiratorially.

"It's cool, isn't it?" he agreed appreciatively, if a bit irreverently for our surroundings, but perhaps solemnity was not always required in this space. Faith was supposed to be a joyous thing, was it not? Then, too, I would probably be less awed if it fell to me to mop the floor and clean the bathrooms. I returned his grin, gave him a thumbs-up, and scooted back down the stairs to regain my seat at the back of the lower level just as Sister Marguerite concluded her remarks and retreated down the aisle to join me.

"It was too long, wasn't it?" she self-critiqued her presentation.

"It didn't seem long at all to me," I answered honestly, although something a friend had once told me about sins of omission niggled at my conscience.

Jeff was Michael's brother's son, and Michael and I were his godparents, "although what business a nonbeliever like me has calling herself a godmother is beyond me," I remember telling Michael. "Couldn't I just be his devoted auntie?"

But Jeff's mother was a staunch Catholic, so godmother it must be. I presented myself at the church on the appointed day for the prayers and the wetting of the head, but my involvement with the child from that point on had been minimal. We presented Jeff with gifts at Christmas and on his birthday, and we put together a nice collection of savings bonds that he ultimately converted to a down payment on a car, and that was about it.

Still, over the years I enjoyed seeing Jeff at the endless family functions to which Michael's kin subjected me. Truth to tell, I enjoyed very few of my in-laws, but Jeff's intelligence and quirky way of looking at the world always appealed to me. He was too uncoordinated to be athletic, a fact of life he accepted philosophically, if a bit wistfully, but throughout high school, he was the mainstay of both the debating team and the chess club. His nice-but-average looks didn't make him the class heartthrob, but his quick wit and dry sense of humor kept the girls giggling.

"I may be a geek, Aunt Kate," he had told me once, "but I can always get a hot date for the dance." I suspected that the girls who accepted Jeff's invitations as a lark had been surprised to find themselves having a very good time.

One of Jeff's hot dates had been Donna. When her football-playing boyfriend was injured senior year and couldn't take her to the big autumn dance, he recruited Jeff to take his place. "It was the worst play he ever made," Jeff confided to me that Christmas. Donna had shyly accompanied him to the inevitable family gathering. "She's the one. She doesn't know it yet, but she's stuck with me for life."

At the time, I had smiled at his unrealistic confidence about the way things would turn out, but here we were, seven years later, preparing for their wedding.

"It's so good of you to do this for us," Donna said to me. She and Jeff sat with me at the kitchen table. We were waiting for the caterer, who was finally making an in-person visit to tell us how he wanted things arranged before the arrival of his crew on Sunday.

"Not at all," I assured her. "It's a Schmidt tradition to be married at home, and Michael and Sheila just can't manage it in that apartment. I'm glad to help."

"So it's Aunt Kate to the rescue," Jeff grinned. Now a fast-tracker at one of New York's most prestigious accounting firms, he had lost none of his impish appeal. I winked at him.

"The most reliable agnostic godmother in the East, that's me. Besides, if this caterer is as good as Michael says he is, there won't be anything for me to do but get out of the way."

"I hope so. Speaking of Uncle Mike, we were sorry when things didn't work out for the two of you." His ears reddened slightly.

"Not to worry," I said lightly. "We had twenty-two good years, raised two great kids, and we're still friends. Michael and Sheila are crazy about each other, as are Armando and I. There's nothing to complain about from where I sit."

The two youngsters were obviously relieved to hear it. "Where is Armando?" Donna asked. "I had looked forward to meeting him tonight."

"California on business, but he'll be here for the wedding." *I hope,* I added silently. I looked closely at Donna. She seemed pale and tired, not unusual for a bride-to-be but unusual for her normal, vivacious self.

"Are you feeling all right?" I asked, putting a hand on her arm. "You look a little tired."

"Oh, she's more than tired," Jeff announced. "She's knocked up like a cheerleader, and won't that give everyone something to talk about at the wedding?"

Donna and I exchanged knowing looks. "These days, not so much," I told him. "Sorry to disappoint you. You're happy about this?" I asked Donna.

"Over the moon," she assured me, "just a little nauseated."

"I remember," I sympathized. "Can I offer you a cracker?"

"That would be great."

As I rose to fetch the Wheat Thins, the doorbell rang, and Jeff went to let in the caterer.

I spent a largely sleepless night, tossing and turning, my mind whirling with the emotions of the day. I cuddled my old cat to me. She accepted the warmth laconically, as she accepted most things these days, showing no interest, no spark of life. My eyes burned with unshed tears at the possibility of losing my old girl so soon after Simon had left me, however unwillingly. I reached for the telephone on the bedside table, needing to talk to Armando.

"Is something the matter?" Armando asked as soon as he recognized the phone number and picked up. I was so close to tears, I couldn't immediately speak.

"Are you ill? What is it, *Mia*?" I could hear him thrashing his way out from under his bedcovers and struggling to sit up. I realized it was still the middle of the night in California.

I cleared my throat, contrite at having awakened him but needing to hear his voice too much to let that matter.

"Armando," was all I could manage at first.

"I'm here, *Cara*. Tell me."

I listened to him breathing, pictured him clutching the phone in his darkened hotel room. I closed my eyes and imagined that I was there with him, dozing cozily under the warm covers, inhaling his clean, soapy scent. It was enough to stop my heart's crazy pounding. I tried again.

"I'm all right, Armando. At least, I'm not sick, or does being heartsick count? Because I certainly am that." Once begun, I couldn't seem to stop. "Everything is such a mess. James O'Halloran is still missing, and his wife thinks he's run off with a former lover who had a child by him. Emma is besotted with some young hunk that Joey thinks is cheating on her. Strutter seems to have disappeared off the face of the earth, and now I'm going to have to wrestle with that stupid goose by myself. Jasmine is hanging on by a thread, and on Sunday, Jeff and Donna are getting married here, and the caterer doesn't like our house much. It wasn't even the big cheese himself who showed up tonight. It was some officious little gnome with a big clipboard who kind of sneered at everything I showed him and kept saying everything had to be perfect for the boss on Sunday," I concluded my litany of misery.

Silence. Then, "What is going on with Jasmine?" As usual, Armando sifted through the superficial grievances and focused on the matter of most importance.

"She's pining. She won't eat. I haven't heard her purr since you left. She misses you."

"*She* misses me?" I could hear the teasing smile in his voice, but I wasn't so far gone that I would admit to being a complete basket case without him.

"The vet says we should get another cat to give her a new interest in life."

"So we shall," he said equably. "Unfortunately, there is no shortage of homeless felines, as we both know."

"How can I do that, Armando? How can I go to one of those shelters and choose just one to come home with us, leave the others behind?"

"I will help you, and we will hope that the others soon have their chance," Armando soothed.

We were quiet for a moment. Nothing had really changed in the last five minutes, and yet everything had.

"Why is it necessary for you to wrestle with a goose?" Armando changed gears. His understanding of English idioms sometimes failed him. I smiled to myself but wasn't ready to laugh.

"It's in the Martha Stewart handbook on staging the perfect Christmas Eve," I told him. "Don't worry about it. I can handle it."

Armando chuckled. "I am quite certain that you can. I have complete faith in you." I could hear the sudden weariness in his voice. My conscience smote me for having wakened him. "Will you be all right until I get there?" he murmured drowsily.

"Depends. When will that be, exactly?"

"Just as soon as I can find an empty seat on a plane flying east. It is Christmas, you know."

"Believe me," I sighed, "no one knows that better than I do. Go back to sleep."

Eight

Armando and I had a long history. Following my amicable divorce from Michael some ten years ago, I had settled happily into my single existence. Emma and Joey had been safely launched, so I had no one but myself and my two old cats to worry about. Quite frankly, it was heaven.

I have always been content in my own company and don't understand people who are uncomfortable going places alone. A newspaper or whatever book I'm currently reading makes perfect company in a coffee shop or restaurant, and if I don't like a movie after the first half-hour, I enjoy being able to leave, if I've gone by myself. Without someone else's preferences or schedule to consider, I was free to go where I wanted, when I wanted, outside of the constraints of my job.

At that time, I was the marketing manager of a small but growing telecommunications company called, appropriately enough, TeleCom, Inc. The fact that my job was hectic and frustrating only added to my enjoyment of my peace and solitude at the end of every day.

The one thing I did not choose to do after the divorce was date. I simply had no interest in pursuing the inevitable romantic entanglements that dating engendered. It might have been pleasant to share an evening with an attractive man or two, but the experiences of my women friends in that area had taught me that dating—just dating—was a tricky business. The men to whom one was attracted were invariably elusive, but those one found far less appealing almost always presumed an attachment one did not feel. Complications, hurt feelings, and general emotional chaos ensued.

Far better, I decided, to remain footloose and fancy free, and for several years, I did just that. Then Armando came to work as TeleCom's new comptroller.

Because investor relations was a large part of my job, our paths crossed frequently. During our meetings to discuss the quarterly reports to the Securities Exchange Commission and various other government agencies, I couldn't help but notice Armando's Latin good looks and delightfully accented baritone. His gentlemanly manners were also a definite plus. I was aware that he was single, but since romantic entanglements were off my agenda, I really didn't think about him in that way.

It was his mischievous sense of humor that finally did me in.

"What do you mean?" Strutter probed, as our waitress put steaming cups of coffee on the table before us. Strutter had resurfaced after three days of nursing her husband through the flu. We had agreed to meet at the diner, since I didn't have to be at the UCC until one o'clock. Baby Olivia napped obligingly in her rocker chair. From time to time, she sucked furiously on her pacifier, frowning in concentration. "Did he play a practical joke on you or something?"

I smiled as I remembered what had so captivated me. "No, nothing like that. It was around this time of year, as a matter of fact, just before Christmas. I asked him if he missed being in South America, or if he had he gotten used to our American way of celebrating Christmas. He assured me that he was totally acclimated. As a silly sort of test, I asked him if he could name Santa's reindeer."

Strutter looked thoughtful as she sipped her coffee. "Gee, I don't think I could do that. It's like the Seven Dwarves. You think you know them until somebody asks you to name them, and then you bog down after four or five." She raised an eyebrow.

"Dasher, Dancer, Prancer, Vixen, Comet, Cupid, Donner, Blitzen," I answered her unspoken question.

She grinned. "Good thing I didn't put money on that bet. So how did Armando do with your little quiz?"

"He didn't even hesitate. He looked me right in the eye and said, 'Flasher, Rainbow, Pretzel...' and I don't know what else, because I completely cracked up."

Strutter looked as if she had somehow missed the joke. "That was it? That was what captured your heart?"

"You had to be there," I assured her, but she remained skeptical.

"After that?"

"After that, we had lunch a couple of times and then dinner a couple of times ..."

"Then wild, crazy sex a couple of times."

I smiled into my coffee cup.

"So last year you moved in together. What comes next?"

I looked at her innocently, pretending not to understand.

"When's the wedding?" she demanded in exasperation.

"You know my feelings on that subject."

"Uh huh." She twitched Olivia's blanket into place. "I also know that feelings change. I wasn't in the market for a second husband when my John came along, and you were determined to avoid men altogether, as I recall." She shrugged. "Stuff happens, and you change your mind."

As usual, she was perceptive almost to the point of clairvoyance. I often kidded her about her Jamaican ancestry, remarking that she would have made a splendid Obeah-woman. "We've talked about it," I admitted now.

"We all know that, but it's been a heck of a long conversation. Come on, spill it." She leaned forward, and I held up my hands to ward her off.

"Whoa, slow down. There's nothing to spill. We just decided that we both needed some time to be sure that's what we want to do, that's all."

"How much time?"

I rolled my eyes. "I believe we said we'd give it a year."

"When was that?"

The woman was a pit bull. I put my cup carefully into its saucer. "It was a year ago, okay?"

"Aha, I knew it! I just had a feeling it was time," she said happily.

I couldn't help but smile along with her. "You could be right. I thought I would enjoy having my solitude back this week while Armando is traveling, but I've missed him like crazy."

"That's how it happens," she said with satisfaction. "They drive you absolutely nuts half the time, and then when they're not around, you miss them. It's the damnedest thing."

"It is that," I agreed, "but I can't even begin to think about my own wedding until I get Jeff's and Donna's done."

"Oh, man, I almost forgot about that. The Christmas Eve production for Emma and the boyfriend isn't bad enough. You have to host a wedding in your house on Sunday."

"Well, hosting is a bit of an overstatement," I amended in the interest of accuracy. "Michael and Sheila have really done the planning, and there's a local caterer who's doing the heavy lifting. I'm just providing the house, is all."

"Minister or Justice of the Peace?" Strutter asked. She put down her cup and pressed one hand to her midsection.

"J.P. What's the matter with your stomach?"

"I don't know. It's probably nothing, but I surely don't want any more coffee." She looked at her watch. "I think

Olivia and I had better hit the road anyway. She has a check-up at eleven-thirty, and we don't want to keep Dr. Peterson waiting."

As if on cue, Olivia awakened from her nap. Instead of fussing, as most infants do when coming out of sleep, she let her pacifier drop neatly onto her blanket and smiled at her mom.

"It figures you would get the perfect baby," I commented as we gathered our belongings and headed for the door. "Does this child ever give you a bad time?"

"You bet," Strutter replied cheerfully, "especially when she's teething. She's cutting a tooth right now, as a matter of fact. She wailed like a banshee all last night. I was afraid she was coming down with that awful flu John had, but nope, it was just a tooth."

We packed up quickly and headed in opposite directions after leaving the diner. After taking care of a couple of pressing errands, I headed into Hartford under low clouds that threatened snow. I would arrive a bit before my appointed time, but if I got through the pile of paperwork that waited on my desk, I planned to treat myself to an hour or so of the open rehearsal for the Christmas Eve services at the Cathedral. Sister Marguerite had told me about it the previous day.

"The midnight mass is solemn and impressive, to be sure," she had told me just yesterday, "but the early mass with the little ones and the families of every color and configuration … ah, 'tis something to see, Katie, and the music!" She clasped her hands in rapture. "I know you're not a believer, though we're working on that, but I know you've a soft spot for the music," she twinkled at me over the top of her reading spectacles. I felt heat flood my face.

"You don't miss much, do you, Sister?" I squirmed in embarrassment.

"'twouldn't be the first time someone slipped out during one of my reports. I can just about keep from nodding off myself," she chuckled. "So if music is the chink in your armor, I'm not above taking advantage of it. You get yourself over to the Cathedral late tomorrow afternoon for the choir rehearsal. We're locking up here at three o'clock, and you can skedaddle right on over."

"Won't anyone mind my just strolling in?" Even to my agnostic sensibilities, it seemed blasphemous to intrude on such an occasion.

"Bless you, child, no one will even notice you among all the singers and musicians."

"Musicians? That magnificent organ isn't enough?"

"Not on Christmas, no, indeed. There's a string quartet and a small brass ensemble, as well. You know what they say. We Catholics know how to put on a good show, isn't that right, Aloysius?" Her full-throated laugh rang out, and the old poodle's tail thumped merrily in agreement. "As I started to say, besides all of the performers, the rehearsal is open to the public. Lots of folks, especially the old ones who don't like to venture out after dark, will be there. You'll simply be one of the crowd," she assured me. "So go find yourself some Christmas."

I remembered her words as I crept from traffic light to

traffic light along Asylum Avenue. Here I was, surrounded by some of the most venerable churches in Hartford. Each and every one of them was in an ecstasy of preparation for the anniversary of Christ's birth, the real Christmas. Yet even in the midst of such joy, miles from the frenzied commercialism which so depressed me, I still could not get into the spirit of the season. Armando was so far away. My daughter was ensnared in a one-sided love affair that was certain to turn out badly. Every second person I talked to had at least one family member down with the flu. The Wadsworth gala had turned into an unspeakable tragedy. Even my old cat was inconsolable.

In the face of all that, I doubted that a few carols, however expertly performed, would turn the season around for me. Still, I looked forward to the rehearsal as a bright spot in an otherwise dreary day.

I worked steadily through the correspondence, grant applications and questionnaires from funding agencies that had accumulated since the previous day. Once again, I marveled at the amount of paperwork that was involved in the charity business. Identifying appropriate funders and preparing grant applications was just the tip of the iceberg. Any contract that was awarded came with a multitude of requirements, each of which necessitated reams of documentation for compliance purposes. I had thought that the law firm for which Margo, Strutter and I had all worked a few years back took top honors for paper consumption, but the UCC left it in the dust.

True to her word, Sister Marguerite shooed the staff on

our way at three o'clock. We wished each other a pleasant holiday with as much manufactured cheer as we could muster, unplugged the Christmas tree in the conference room, set the security alarm, and filed out into the darkening afternoon.

The snow which had been threatening all day had begun to fall in fat, wet flakes that quickly coated the cars in the parking lot. Everyone else scurried for home and the million and one details still requiring their attention, but I headed for the back entrance of the Cathedral on the other side of the parking lot. *Just one hour,* I promised myself, *and then I'll go home and face the preparations for my Christmas Eve ordeal.*

As usual, the sheer presence of the Cathedral inspired my admiration, but it was the music that raised goose bumps on my arms as soon as the door shut behind me. I climbed the stairs quietly to the main level, pulled upward by the tones emanating from the majestic Austin organ. This time, it accompanied the Cathedral choir, which was practicing the Christmas section of Handel's *Messiah.* I hoped I had not missed a run-through of the "Hallelujah Chorus" from that stirring work.

Although not full, by any means, many of the pews were occupied. I slipped into a seat on the right, near the confessionals that lined the wall. Looking around as the music director instructed the choir on a tricky passage, I was surprised to see a light on above one of the curtained booths. I presumed that meant it was in use. Apparently, the work of saving souls must continue, Christmas or not. I had no knowledge of what transpired between priest and confessor, but if the movies were to be trusted, eventually the curtain would open, and the penitent would find his or her way to an open pew. There, he or she would utter prayers of atonement. *How wonderful it must be to be so easily freed of guilt for one's unworthy thoughts and deeds,* I mused. *We nonbelievers must just muddle on, doing the best we can from day to day and hoping we get it right occasionally.*

A brisk countdown from the director, accompanied by a signal for the choir to stand, recaptured my wandering attention, and I sat forward as the organ boomed out the introduction to the hoped-for chorus. As always, the jubilant harmonies elated me, as they had everyone who heard them in the two hundred plus years since Handel had composed them. I thought about the thousands, if not millions, of singers throughout the world who would thrill to the masterpiece over the next few days. *What a gift,* I thought yet again, *to be able to create a work of such splendor to uplift the spirits of those who came after you in perpetuity.*

"Divine inspiration, you might say," Sister Marguerite inserted herself into my thoughts, and I smiled in spite of myself. I would leave that door open to appease her.

As the piece reached its final crescendo, the curtain on the confessional flicked open. Its occupant emerged, a middle-aged man wearing a rather dirty raincoat, his head bowed. The appreciative listeners around me burst into spontaneous applause as the confessor dragged himself down the outer aisle instead of seating himself in a pew, as I had expected. He appeared oblivious to the applause.

Keeping his head low, he pulled up the collar of the shabby raincoat and headed for the door through which I had entered.

He probably prefers to do his praying in private, I thought absently, clapping enthusiastically with the others as the director made a sweeping bow. *Who can blame him? Anyone who has sins grievous enough to drive him into the confessional in the midst of all this festivity must have a heavy burden to lay down.* The man's face, what little I could see of it above the raincoat collar, was pale and drawn, his whole demeanor inexpressibly weary. He reminded me a little of someone, but I couldn't think who.

As the tumultuous applause died down, a young priest stepped from the confessional into the aisle and stood looking after the retreating figure. His face registered conflicting emotions, none of them good. Then I knew who the man in the raincoat reminded me of.

Nine

Christmas Eve morning, and my nose was in Strutter's cookbook once again. This time, I was seeking roasting instructions for the turkey sitting in my sink. I had already dealt with the, eww, giblets, rinsed the thing, and patted it dry. The cavity had been salted, peppered, and stuffed with pieces of carrot, onion and celery. Now I was instructed to "place the bird on a roasting rack in a shallow pan, and roast at a temperature of three hundred twenty-five degrees for twenty minutes per pound or until the juices run clear when a knife is inserted between the leg and the body."

Besides being totally grossed out by all this talk of cavities and juices and bodies, I had no idea in the world what a roasting rack might be. Any chicken that had ever had occasion to find its way into my oven had been plopped straight into a roasting pan, thanks very much. As for poundage, all I knew was that I had asked for a turkey weighing between twelve and fifteen pounds, which Strutter had told me was the smallest I could expect to find. That was just before she hung up on me the previous evening.

"Charlie and Olivia came down with the flu," she had moaned, "and I don't feel so good myself, to tell you the truth. Sorry, but you're on your own. Good luck." And she was gone.

On her advice, I had abandoned the goose idea as being too tricky for a beginner to manage. With apologies to the wild birds who even now bobbed in a cautious parade across my lawn, I had driven straight to the Bliss Market first thing this morning and stood in line at the butcher counter for the better part of an hour. I was convinced that every matron in Wethersfield had pre-ordered the meat for her Christmas dinner here, and today was pick-up day. It was enough to make a vegetarian out of anyone.

"Believe me, Miss, this is the last fresh turkey available in Connecticut," the harassed butcher informed me when at last it was my turn. "I can only let you have it because the customer who ordered it is down with …"

" … the flu," I finished for him. "Yes, there's a lot of that going around."

"It's a little bigger than you want." He held it up for inspection. Its naked wings flapped obscenely.

"Wrap it up," I said, more to get it out of my sight than anything else. Now here it was, taking up most of my sink. The question was, how many pounds constituted "a little bigger" than I had asked for?

After staring bleakly at the thing for several minutes, I called Margo. As usual, she had the answer.

"Weigh yourself on the bathroom scale while carryin' it, Sugar. Then subtract your weight, and bingo. You doin' okay with all of this?"

"I'll manage," I assured her. "If Strutter can deal with a sick son and baby, I can roast a damned turkey. Thanks for the tip."

Grimly, I wrapped the carcass in a kitchen towel and traipsed into the bathroom, where I stepped onto the scale. My heart almost stopped at the figure on the display. Either I had gained several pounds since Armando's departure, or this was one major turkey. I put the bird on the vanity and stepped back on the scale. The good news was, I hadn't put on any weight. The bad news was, the turkey weighed eighteen pounds. At twenty minutes a pound, that was six hours of roasting. I hoped I could afford to pay my utility bill at the end of the month.

While attempting to execute the approved wing tuck maneuver, whereby the skinny ends of the wings were bent unnaturally behind the body of the bird, I distinctly heard a bone snap. I knew it was the turkey's, not mine, but it was still enough to make my stomach lurch. I scrabbled through the lower cupboards in search of something that might serve as a roasting rack and came up with the one on which I had cooled cakes and cookies twenty years ago when I still made such things for the kids. Reasoning that a rack was a rack, I fitted it into the bottom of the roasting pan and dropped the turkey on top of it. By the time I had wrestled the whole thing into the oven, I was ready for a glass of wine and a nap. Since it was only nine-thirty in the morning. I settled for a cup of coffee and dialed Emma's number. I was going through this torture for her. Why should she be allowed to sleep in?

"He's on his way!" she greeted me cheerfully.

"Santa and his sleigh? I thought that only happened after the kiddies are all asleep," I countered with forced silliness. "Oh, you mean Jared, don't you?"

"You know perfectly well I do. According to his text message last night, he'll be on the highway by noon. The drive is four to five hours, depending on the traffic, so he should be here by five o'clock at the latest."

"He sent you a text message? You mean, you haven't talked to him? What happened to actual conversations, or am I just hopelessly behind the times?"

"He just didn't have enough time to call. All the kids were being picked up by the parents yesterday, and there was a farewell thing in the afternoon. It was just one thing after another, you know," Emma dismissed my questions a shade too brightly for my liking. *One thing after another, or one girl after another?* I wondered uncharitably. *I mean, there's a whole evening unaccounted for here.* Somehow, I held my tongue.

"Have you talked to Joey today? I don't even know when he and Justine are getting here."

"Umm, yeah, we talked." Now she was really hedging. "I don't know about their plans, though. He said Justine wasn't feeling very well."

I groaned. "If I hear about one more case of the flu, I think I'm going to scream, but I'll give them a call to see what's going on," I promised. "Somebody had better show up to eat this great hulking turkey."

"Turkey? I thought we were having roast goose?" Emma had the nerve to sound dismayed. "Turkey isn't as traditional as roast goose, is it?"

My temper rose dangerously close to the red zone. "What with one thing or another, Em, the goose thing didn't work out, so Jared will just have to make do," I managed after mentally counting to ten. "So who's bringing the chestnuts to roast on the fire?"

She forced a laugh. "I guess that's another thing we'll have to do without. Sorry, Momma. I know I'm being a pain about this, and you're a saint to put up with me. It's just that it's so important for everything to be perfect."

I knew it would be wiser not to pursue this unlikely line of reasoning from my usually level-headed daughter but found I could not resist. "I don't understand why it's so important, Emma. Why does everything have to be perfect for this guy? You've never given a fig about this sort of thing before. You've always been a take-me-as-I-am kind of person, and there have been plenty of fellows willing to do just that. Frankly, I find this whole thing a little alarming." I struggled to soften my tone. "You're just not acting like yourself, Sweetie."

She was quiet for several seconds. Then, "I know what you're saying. I wish I had an answer for you. I know I'm acting weird, and you're right, it isn't like me to care so much, but I do. I just can't help it, Momma. I guess it's just hormones," she added, baiting me a little.

I was so happy to hear her say something that reminded me of the old Emma that I capitulated. Is there a woman alive who hasn't been irrationally besotted at one time or another? If my down-to-earth daughter was having her turn, then I would do what I could to support her. I just wished this Jared person didn't sound like such a jerk.

"Probably is," I agreed equably, "but I guess you're entitled to be in lust at least once. See you later, Dearie."

I sat over my cooling coffee for another ten minutes and then got up to shower off the smell of raw turkey. The hot spray felt wonderful, and I stood under it until it started to cool, a sure sign that the hot water heater had reached its limits. Quickly, I lathered up and sluiced off the suds.

After blowing my hair dry and donning a presentable sweater-and-slacks outfit, I felt restored enough to call my son. The call went immediately to voice mail, which wasn't unusual, considering Joey's odd work hours. When he needed to sleep, he just turned off his cell phone. Justine had her own phone, which I tried next with the same result. Well, it was Christmas Eve, so both she and Joey probably had the day off from work. Perhaps they were both sleeping or doing a little Christmas shopping. I reminded myself that whatever they were doing, it was none of my business. I just hoped they were happy doing it. Unlike Emma's present romantic relationship, I was optimistic about Joey and his live-in love. She seemed to be a strong, intelligent young woman, capable of handling whatever nonsense my irrepressible son dished out, and I wished the two of them well.

By mid-afternoon, I had prepared enough food to feed a small village. Margo stopped by after some last-minute shopping for a restorative cup of tea. She parked her slim haunches on a stool at the pass-through counter between my kitchen and dining room and surveyed my handiwork with something akin to awe.

"How many people did you say you're feedin'?" She gazed at a pan of sausage-and-apple stuffing, ready to go into the oven, another of candied yams, and a covered green bean casserole. Then she flicked her eyes toward the table laden with pumpkin and apple pies, plates of cookies, and a coconut layer cake.

"Don't know," I said dully. I slouched in exhaustion in the big easy chair in the living room, a mug of tea on my chest. "The way it looks right now, it could be just Emma, Jared, Joey and me. He called a little while ago to say Justine's down sick. Armando's among the missing. He hasn't answered his phone all day."

Margo picked up her tea and came to join me. She gestured at the fireplace, which was dark and cold. "What, no cracklin' blaze on the hearth?"

"I know, I know. I still have to drag in the firewood, and the table has to be set, which means ironing a tablecloth, assuming I can find one."

"This is one hell of a lot of work for dinner for four people," Margo sympathized. "I hope Emma appreciates what she's puttin' her mama through."

"Oh, I'm sure she does," I said, although I had my doubts. "What are you and John doing tonight?"

She hugged herself in anticipation. "Well, since John's parents went to their final reward some years back, and I'm happy to say mine are more than a thousand miles south of here in Atlanta, John's takin' me to dinner at Spris. It's that wonderful Italian restaurant on Constitution Plaza that has floor-to-ceilin' windows overlookin' all those twinklin' lights." The Hartford Festival of Lights was a mainstay of the local holiday season. At dusk on the Friday after Thanksgiving, huge crowds gathered on the plaza to sing carols and watch as thousands upon thousands of tiny white lights were lighted, transforming the scene into a winter wonderland.

"It sounds perfect," I said, meaning it. "How's Strutter doing? I haven't talked with her since yesterday, and things weren't looking too good then."

Margo smiled. "Don't you worry about Strutter. Her mama arrived this mornin' from the island, sized up the situation, and took charge. I'm positive that at this very moment, everyone at the Putnam household is bathed, fed, and tucked up in clean sheets, and Mrs. Tuttle is havin' the time of her life."

In the way that words sometimes do, the phrase "time of her life" sent my thoughts skittering to poor Mary O'Halloran, who had planned to be having the time of her life on a glorious cruise right about now. Instead, she waited alone by her phone, praying for news of her missing husband.

"Still nothing on James O'Halloran?" I asked Margo.

"I almost forgot to tell you. The police traced that Roberta gal, the one James had his unfortunate affair with. She actually lives in California, and yes, there is a son, Patrick, as a result of that relationship. He's about seven and cute as the devil."

I stared at her. Even for Margo, this was information gathering elevated to an art form. "Now how would you know what the child looks like?" I wondered aloud.

"Oh, there are pictures, you know," she said evasively. "They come in for the file, and John sometimes brings work home with him and leaves things lyin' around." She busied herself looking for a tissue in her purse.

"Uh huh. So I gather the police have questioned Roberta about James' disappearance. Was she the woman who called him last Thursday morning?"

"She was," Margo picked up the story eagerly, "but not because she was lookin' for James." She paused for full dramatic effect. "She wanted to know if James had heard from Joseph."

"She knows Joseph O'Halloran?" In my fatigued state, I seemed unable to grasp the meaning of what Margo was trying to tell me.

"Way better'n that, Sugar. She and Joseph O'Halloran are married, or were married, I guess I should say. Roberta is Joseph O'Halloran's widow."

"Wow," I breathed, stunned by this unexpected turn of events. "Does Mary know any of this yet?"

"All of it," Margo assured me. "Gentleman that he is, my John went over there and told her himself. See, James is Joseph's next of kin, legally speakin', and since James can't be located, it falls to Mary as his sister-in-law to make the final arrangements for Joseph. But now that Roberta has been identified as Joseph's legal wife, Mary is off the hook."

I blinked at Margo as my tired brain reeled. I finished my tea and struggled to my feet. "I have no idea what to make of everything you just told me about the O'Hallorans, but I'm glad to hear that Strutter is being looked after by somebody else for a change. I guess some women really do enjoy all this fuss. Personally, I do not see the attraction of cooking all day to produce a meal that will be eaten and forgotten in twenty minutes, then spending two hours cleaning up the kitchen." I looked at the array of edibles before me and felt a wave of revulsion. "I am sick of the sight of food and the smell of food. It's in my clothes. It's in my hair. At this moment, I don't care if I never eat again." I trudged to the sink mutinously. Then I had a thought. "Maybe I could tell Emma I've got the flu. There's so much of it going around."

Margo bumped me aside good-naturedly to rinse her mug out under the faucet. "Then you would have gone through all of this for no good reason. Besides, what would you do with that eighteen-pound turkey?"

"I don't know what I'm going to do with it now except hope that the kids take home lots of leftovers."

Margo washed my mug and added it to hers on the

drainboard. "Cheer up, Sugar. It's just one evenin', and your man will be home soon."

"You think?"

She nodded. "I have a good feelin' about it. She gave me a hug and shrugged into her stylish pants coat. "It'll all be over soon. Go take a nap."

I took Margo's advice and joined Jasmine on my bed for a nap. I lay on my side and cuddled her to me for maximum warmth on her old bones. To be sure I wouldn't oversleep, I set the alarm clock for four-thirty. That would give me time to finish up the food and build a fire in the fireplace. I eschewed the table cloth idea and decided to go with a buffet. In five minutes flat, I was sound asleep.

Thinking that the alarm had awakened me, I sat up with a start. Jasmine snored on, oblivious, as I stretched across her to look at the clock. Four-fifteen.

"Momma?" Emma stood wavering in the doorway of my bedroom, having come in through the garage as I slept. She looked absolutely ghastly. My first thought was that she was ill, and I rushed to her. I looked closely at her face and was appalled by what I saw there. She had obviously taken pains with her appearance, but no amount of mascara or eyeliner in the world could disguise her red-rimmed eyes and the dark circles beneath them, much less her bleak expression. Her skin was papery, her hands clammy. I pulled her to the end of the bed and sat down next to her, holding her cold hands in both my own.

"What is it, Emma? Tell me."

The empty eyes lifted to meet mine. "He's not coming," she said. "Jared's not coming tonight or any other night, for that matter. He sent me an email a couple of hours ago. There's another girl, someone local. He's sorry, he said, and I should try not to hate him."

I was devastated for my strong, beautiful daughter who had never before experienced this particular sort of pain. When it came to love affairs, Emma had always called the shots. I had never before seen her heartbroken, and it was terrible to see. There was no worse pain, I knew, and I was filled with rage for the arrogant young stud who had done this to my daughter. Helpless to assuage her grief in any real way, I did what we always did in tough spots, she and I.

"Well, at least he didn't break up with you on a Post-it," I said.

It took Emma all of two seconds to connect my *non sequitur* to an episode of *Sex and the City,* a television show we had both followed avidly, in which the heroine's latest swain had done just that. Her lips twitched, and a small gleam enlivened her glazed eyes.

"Jackass," I said.

"Scumbag," she agreed.

"Weasel."

"Bastard." I let her have the last word, and we both burst into laughter. That, in turn, triggered the tears she still needed to shed. I held her head and rubbed her back as she sobbed, the age-old comforts of touch and shared experience that a mother could offer a daughter. There was really nothing else I could do.

While I patted and cooed and passed fresh tissues from the box on my bedside table, my thoughts drifted back to a painful love affair of my own back in the day, when I had lived in California for a couple of years. It had been intense, all-consuming, and when he told me it was over, it was the end of my world. Not knowing where else to go or what else to do, I returned to New England to lick my wounds, where I met and married Michael and raised a family with him. Although we grew apart and eventually divorced, I had been fortunate enough to have Armando come into my life. So instead of ending my world, my California lover had freed me to have loving, long-term relationships with two strong, decent men.

I wished there were some way to communicate that experience magically to Emma, whose sobs were subsiding to sniffles and gulps, but I knew she couldn't possibly hear me now. The gut-wrenching grief must first be endured. Only time could give her the necessary perspective to understand the gift she had just been given by the jackass/scumbag/weasel/bastard.

"Oh, Christ," said Joey from the doorway, where he stood surveying the sad little scene with obvious disgust. "Let me guess. The sports stud dumped her."

 **Ten**

By the time they reached their late twenties, Joey and Emma had fallen easily into an adult sibling relationship. Joey was a mere seventeen months older than Emma, but they were very different people. They didn't hang out together. They had different friends and interests, but they were genuinely fond of one another and took pride in each other's accomplishments.

It had not always been that way. Past toddlerhood, when they had been pals and playmates, their relationship had been volatile, to say the least. Both were outspoken and opinionated, traits that inevitably led to contests of will. When they were teenagers, their quarrels were frequent and loud. It was the rare week that didn't include yelling and door-slamming. Occasionally, their brawls got physical. Emma had speed and agility going for her, but Joey had stealth and size on his side.

Watching them now from where I still sat on the edge of my bed was like traveling fifteen years back in time. Joey howled insults at his sister for being so stupid and naïve, and Emma screamed at him to go away and leave her alone. As I had then, I sat back and let them vent, waiting for the best opportunity to step in and separate the combatants before they came to blows.

I was overcome with an inexplicable lassitude. In the face of the very real misery I had witnessed over the past week, this venomous exchange over something as inconsequential as a misguided crush filled me with sadness. Then, suddenly, I had had enough. I stood up and stalked to where they stood at the bedroom door, nose-to-nose, hurling epithets at each other. I put one hand on each of their shoulders to get their attention. They turned to look at me, their eyes blazing.

"That's it," I told them quietly. "That is the last straw. I want you both to leave."

They blinked at me as if I were speaking a foreign language.

"Which word didn't you understand? Go. Right now." I turned them toward the kitchen and hustled them, none too gently, down the hallway.

At this interesting juncture, Armando appeared in the doorway from the garage. The first thing I noticed was that he looked exhausted. The second was the dainty, ginger-colored cat struggling to free herself from the confines of his TeleCom windbreaker, which was zipped firmly beneath her chin. Armando's eyes sought mine, as they did whenever we were reunited after an extended absence, and a smile tugged at the corners of his mouth. Emma and Joey continued to quarrel at top volume, oblivious to Armando's arrival.

"You made it," I finally managed, overwhelmed with love, gratitude and, yes, relief. After days of feeling the emotional sands shifting beneath my feet, I felt solid footing blessedly returning. "Who's your friend?" I pulled him into the hallway and scritched the cat's head gently.

"It is as if our conversation on the phone last evening was overheard. I know you are not ready yet for another cat, *Cara*. You have not finished grieving for your Simon, but this one cannot wait. She needs us now. Also, Jasmine very much needs a new companion. Can you not open your heart for her and for this little one?"

"Where did you find her?"

"I did not. She found me. Someone abandoned her in the airport parking lot. When the shuttle bus dropped me off near my car, she came out from under an S.U.V. and wrapped herself around my ankles. She chose me to help her, and I could not refuse."

A choppy purr emanated from the pumpkin-colored mite, and her eyelids drooped over eyes the color of amber. Armando was correct. I wasn't ready for another cat, but what was I to do? Emma and Joey finally exhausted their sibling rhetoric and gazed at the newcomer silently, then at me. It was clear that I had quickly been outnumbered.

"Welcome to the family," I told the little hairball with resignation. "I sure hope you like turkey."

"Make that extremely well-done turkey," Joey commented, wrinkling his nose at a suspicious odor seeping from the oven. "How long has that thing been roasting anyway?"

"Too long," I replied, not particularly caring. "It doesn't matter now. I really don't care for turkey."

"Well, I do, and I'm starving. At least let me take some home to Justine." Before I could warn him not to, he yanked open the oven door, releasing a cloud of greasy fumes. As I had known they would, all five smoke alarms in the house went off simultaneously.

"The windows!" I shrieked at Emma and Joey after a moment of stunned silence. "Throw open as many as you can while I get rid of this thing."

Armando fled upstairs with the terrified cat, presumably to shut her into his room while we dealt with this latest catastrophe. I slid my hands into oven mitts and grabbed the heavy pan holding the smoking turkey carcass.

"Open the back door, quick," I begged, and Joey sprang to oblige. He held the storm door wide as I eased by him with the ruined bird and deposited it, hissing in the wet snow, on the back deck.

I propped the door open with a deck chair, and we returned inside to help Emma and Armando wrestle open more windows. After what seemed like an eternity, the smoke alarms stuttered, then stopped. *If we ever have a real fire in the middle of the night,* I thought, *we'll be far more likely to have heart attacks from being awakened by these hellacious alarms than to expire from fire or smoke.*

Armando had propped open the front door, as well, to create a clearing draft straight through the house. The four

of us stood shivering in the cold living room. In the
sudden quiet, an obscene, wet pop burst from the turkey
carcass on the deck. Joey snorted.

"Turkey fart," he choked before exploding into
guffaws.

Armando struggled to keep a straight face but quickly
gave up the battle, joining Joey in raucous laughter. Emma
and I exchanged eye rolls. *Boys will be boys.* She trudged
upstairs to begin closing windows while I went to shut the
doors. The men made a half-hearted attempt to deal with
the downstairs windows, still chortling and wiping their
eyes.

Jasmine, roused from her endless nap not by the noise,
thanks to her deafness, but by the strange smells and drop
in temperature, came into the room, sniffing madly, which
was when we all remembered the cat shut in Armando's
room. The poor thing probably wished herself back in the
airport parking lot.

"Oh, boy, have we got a surprise for you," I told
Jasmine, scooping her up and ruffling her fur, "but first,
let's get this fireplace going."

An hour later, stuffed with candied yams and green bean
casserole, we considered and rejected dessert. The ginger
cat, having been fed and shown the litter box, hid behind
the sofa. Jasmine lay on her pillow before the fire, quiet but
alert for a possible sneak attack by the newcomer.

"At least she's not asleep," I observed, leaning

contentedly against Armando where we sat together on the sofa.

"Which is more than can be said about Armando," Emma pointed out. I turned my head to look at him sleeping soundly where he sat. It had been a long flight and an eventful day.

"I've never understood how he can sleep sitting up," I mused.

"I do it all the time. Justine says I sleep better in the recliner than I do in bed," Joey chimed in.

"It has to be a guy thing. Show them a good time, fill their bellies, and they fall asleep on you every time," Emma concluded with her old sassiness. "Well, as much fun as this has been, I think I'll go have a drink with Lori and David. They're having some people over tonight, and I'm invited." She consulted her watch. "Good grief. It's not even nine o'clock." She scrambled to her feet and looked at her brother. "Feel like coming along?"

Well, well, I thought, *the ultimate peace offering.*

"Thanks, but I think I'd better get back to my old lady," Joey replied. "The flu's made her cranky enough already. Besides, I don't want to have to witness you taking all the abuse they're going to give you about Jared. I might have to defend your honor or something." His eyes conveyed more sympathy than his gruff words, a fact which was not lost on Emma, I felt certain.

"Yeah, well, I might as well get it over with," was her mild reply. "They all told me ... *you* all told me," she corrected herself, "that Jared was bad news right from the start. I may as well wash down the crow I'm going to have to eat with some decent champagne. I can always crash there for the night. Come on. Help me clean up these dishes before we go."

Her brother got to his feet and helped her collect the detritus from our casual meal in front of the fireplace. The sounds of dishes being rinsed for the dishwasher and their amiable banter drifted in from the kitchen.

"You're not really asleep, right?" I said to Armando.

He smiled but kept his eyes shut. "It is good to hear Emma sounding more like herself, is it not?"

"Believe me, nobody's happier about that than I am." I fell silent, not wanting to blow his cover.

A few minutes later, Emma and Joey departed after whispering goodbyes and kissing my cheek. As glad as I had been to see them, I relished the peace and quiet that filled the house after they left.

"All clear," I told Armando. He opened his eyes but didn't move. "Would you like some dessert now? God knows, there are plenty of choices. I even made a coconut layer cake, if you can believe it. I know Margo couldn't," I chuckled.

"Dessert, yes, but cake is not what I have in mind." He captured my hand in his and brought it to his lips. I began to get his drift.

"I thought you were tired," I teased him.

"I have never been too tired for dessert, *Cara*," he assured me and turned toward me for a lingering kiss.

I had to admit that despite his long day, he seemed

pretty feisty. My own exhaustion seemed to be disappearing, too.

"Well, then, dessert it is," I murmured. "My place or yours?"

"Don't think of it as incarceration. Consider it protective custody," I told the ginger cat. She sat on the floor next to Armando's bed, ready to dart beneath it if she felt threatened. Apparently, she felt threatened a lot, since she spent as much time under the bed as she did on top of it; but despite her surface timidity, I was beginning to see signs of a mischievous spirit.

"At least it is warm and dry. You could still be freezing your *bonita* tail off in that parking lot," Armando reminded her.

We were installing two baby gates, one on top of the other, in the doorway of Armando's bedroom to keep Jasmine away from the newcomer until she could be tested by the vet for feline leukemia and other contagious diseases. The baby gates had been thoughtfully provided this morning by my octogenarian neighbor Mary, who to my knowledge hadn't thrown anything away in decades. Her house looked like a Goodwill store, but I had to admit that her packrat tendencies came in handy from time to time.

"There," I said, having adjusted the tension bar on the topmost gate to my satisfaction. I released it, stepped over the bottom gate to join Armando in the hall, and put it back into position. "You can see out, but you can't get out. More to the point, Jasmine can't get in. You can get used to each other's scents for a couple of days. Then we'll get you tested, and we'll see."

The cat yawned and retreated beneath the edge of the spread, unimpressed with my logic. We were about to start down the stairs when Armando put a hand on my arm and pointed. Sitting at the foot of the staircase like a self-appointed sentinel was our old girl, her tail wrapped tightly around her feet.

"A very good sign, is it not?" said Armando quietly. I nodded.

"Up until last night, she hadn't been out of my room in days except to use the litter box. Your being home improved her outlook, but the new cat has given her a whole new interest in life."

"So we are keeping her?"

I refused to attach myself before I knew her feline leukemia status. The last thing poor old Jasmine needed was an infectious disease. "Jury's still out," I said firmly and led the way to the kitchen for a second cup of coffee.

Having dreaded Christmas for weeks, it was lovely to have Armando safely at home and the day pretty much to ourselves. I had missed him terribly. True, Christmas Eve had been a disaster in many ways, but at least the Jared situation had been resolved, and Emma seemed well on her way to becoming her old self. Margo and Strutter would be relieved to hear it, I knew. I wondered how Margo's restaurant dinner with John had gone last night and whether Strutter and her family were on the road to recovery from the flu, but I knew we would catch up before the day was over. For the moment, it was more than enough to have Armando drinking coffee with me and Jasmine basking in the sunlight at the foot of the stairs, instead of moping in my bedroom.

Against all odds, we had gotten through the events of yesterday relatively unscathed, and the next ordeal, Jeff's and Donna's wedding, was two days away. The situation with the UCC and the O'Hallorans was undeniably tragic, but I had done everything I knew how to do, and now it was up to the professionals to solve the case. Margo's information about Joseph and Roberta being married was startling, to say the least, but then, everything about this sad little saga had been surprising. I certainly had no insights to offer.

Margo and John were enjoying their first Christmas as a married couple, and Strutter's mom had her household well in hand. Emma and Joey would spend today with their father and Sheila. I was officially off duty.

Being with Armando, with nowhere that we were committed to go and no one we were obliged to see, was more Christmas than I had expected this year, and I planned to savor every moment. We took our mugs into the living room and pulled the drapes wide open to enjoy the morning sunshine. After a week of sleet, rain, and spitting snow, Christmas day was a dazzler.

"It is good to be home," said Armando, drawing me close for a coffee-flavored kiss. "Look, *Cara*." He pointed out the window toward the treeline. "Your feathered friends have come to see you."

Three, four, then seven wild turkeys bobbed cautiously across the back lawn, keeping close to the woods.

"They probably think it's safe to come out now that everyone's Christmas dinner is already in the oven," I smiled. I remembered the ruined carcass on the deck. "We'd better get that burned turkey into the garbage before some poor scavenger gets a bone stuck in its throat."

The turkeys heard me open the door to the deck and fluttered in agitation before scuttling into the underbrush.

"Sorry, guys," I apologized. Last night's dinner was exactly where I had deposited it, greasily charred and intact. "I guess even the local wildlife wouldn't touch it," I joked to Armando, who held open the door. A sudden snarling was our only alert before two coyotes, gaunt and leggy, slunk from the woods and made a dash for the deck, intent on the pan I held. I was momentarily stunned. "Drop it!" Armando yelled. He shook the turkey out of my hands and snatched me roughly back into the house. Within seconds, the coyotes were tearing the carcass apart as three more rushed out of the woods to join the fray. We watched, aghast, as they ripped through the eighteen-pound bird as if it were a canary, their yellow eyes gleaming, bones flying in all directions. The coyotes snapped and snarled for perhaps one full minute. Then, as suddenly as they had appeared, they were gone, melting back into the brush along with the wild turkeys.

I looked at the empty roasting pan lying face down in the back yard and considered going outside to retrieve it. *Maybe later,* I decided. *Maybe never.* I turned away from the window. Armando shut the inside door firmly and pulled me close for a hug. "That was interesting," he commented with his usual understatement. "Are you okay?"

"Hey, everybody's got to make a living," I said as lightly as I could manage. "I'd rather they ate our burned turkey than one of the live wild ones."

I straightened up and smiled brightly at him, determined not to let the incident spoil our day. "How about brunch at the diner? They're open today. Then maybe we can catch that new Meryl Streep comedy we've been wanting to see. It would be a good time to go, since everyone else will be doing their Christmas stuff at home today."

"Good idea," Armando agreed, going along with me. "Even you cannot get into too much trouble eating scrambled eggs and watching a movie." He gave me a final pat and went upstairs to get into the shower. I sank into the big easy chair with my back to the window and drew deep breaths. I had had quite enough of the wonders of nature for one morning.

As a rule, Christmas was the one day a year that the diner was closed, but this year, Marianna and her husband, the owners, had decided to experiment with keeping it open. Judging from the line of waiting customers that filled the entryway, the experiment was a success. Nothing like being the only game in town. We were trying to decide whether to leave or wait it out when Marianna spotted us from her post behind the cash register.

"Your friends are already inside," she called out, waving us in. "Yes, Kate, you," she added in response to my puzzled expression.

With apologies to those still waiting, we eeled through the mob and entered the main seating area, where Margo and John occupied a booth along the near wall.

"Marianna assumed we were meeting you. Can we crash your party?"

Margo whooped and jumped up to give Armando a hug before hustling us into the booth and reseating herself next to her husband. I noticed there was no food on the table, just cups and saucers.

"Did you just get here? How on earth did you snag a booth with that crowd in the lobby?" I wanted to know.

"We've been here for quite a while," John sighed. As always, he was immaculately turned out in a cream-colored turtleneck and gray slacks. "I'd settle for coffee, if I were you, because the kitchen is overwhelmed."

As if to illustrate his words, Sherri rushed up to our table bearing a pot of coffee. At her signal, a beleaguered busboy plunked down cups and saucers, which Sherri filled deftly. She refilled Margo's and John's cups before speeding off to the next table. I sympathized with her and the rest of the staff, who wore the same shell-shocked expression on their faces. Clearly, it was possible to have too much of a good thing.

"This is crazy," was Armando's only comment, "but at least the coffee is good."

"It always is," Margo agreed. "That's partly why we keep comin' here. So tell us all about Emma's fella. Was he worth all the fuss and feathers? Did Christmas Eve come up to his standards?"

Armando and I groaned in unison, but by the time we had filled in our friends on the events of the preceding twenty-four hours, a harassed waitress I had never seen before during my regular visits had somehow contrived to take and deliver our orders. I could not imagine how these hard-working people could put in a grueling shift at the diner, then go home to serve a meal to their families, let alone deal with Christmas. For their sakes, I hoped they were all Jewish.

My story of the ruined turkey, complete with smoke alarms and coyote attack, hadn't been especially funny at the time, but my recitation had Margo laughing so hard, she had to wipe her eyes, and fastidious John nearly spit coffee on the table. "Turkey fart," he choked, and we all howled yet again.

"Stop now," Margo gasped, holding her sides. "I can't take anymore. Our quiet little dinner at Spris can't compete with your evenin', although it was absolutely wonderful," she added, putting her hand over her new husband's.

John beamed back at her. "Dessert was spectacular," he agreed.

At the word *dessert*, Armando smiled broadly at me. "It

is always the best part, is it not?"

I grinned at him. "Well, it was certainly better than the turkey. Who's up for a movie? We haven't seen one in ages and thought we'd go see the new Meryl Streep comedy while everyone else in town is doing their Christmas thing."

Margo and John were in. "Might as well make the most of my first Christmas Day off in ten years," said John. "I always used to work that day so the married guys could be with their families, but now, I'm one of them." He didn't look at all unhappy about his change in status.

We made our way out of the diner and consulted a newspaper, the last one in a nearby vending machine. "We can just make the matinee in Plainville, if we get a move on," I reported.

"You'll have to give us an extra minute," John commented, his hand on Margo's shoulder. "Our car doesn't move until Mrs. Harkness here fixes her lipstick." Honestly, the two of them were bordering on downright sappy with all of this billing and cooing.

"I know," I sympathized. "Sometimes I think I've waited half of my adult life while Margo checks her make-up. We'll see you there."

On the way to the theater, I called Strutter's house to check on the invalids and was surprised when Strutter herself answered the phone. "Oh, I wish I could go with you," she moaned before a coughing fit overtook her. "Where is that blasted Kleenex box? Answering the phone is about all Mama will let me do. Says I can do it right from this bed, so that's where I stay. John drops by now and then, and my son was allowed to show me his Christmas loot from the doorway this morning, but I'm not sure I still have a baby. Mama won't allow Olivia anywhere near me. I miss her fat cheeks," she finished mournfully.

"Think of it as a well-earned vacation," I offered in an attempt to mollify her.

She harrumphed. "A vacation is Mai Tais on the beach. A vacation is a big ol' cruise ship with Disney characters and activity directors for the kids. This is just solitary confinement, Girl." She paused to honk into a tissue. "What's going on with the O'Halloran situation?" she asked. "I'm so bored, I exist on other people's drama."

I spent the rest of the ride filling her in on the latest about Roberta and Joseph O'Halloran, while she continued to cough and blow her nose. "Don't worry about Vista Views," I finished up. "Nothing happens during the week between Christmas and New Year's anyway, and Margo will keep an eye on things, if she can tear herself away from John for ten minutes."

Strutter chuckled. "Still honeymooning, huh?"

"*Ad nauseam*," I confirmed. "You take care of yourself."

We pulled into the parking lot at the Plainville 20 Theaters in good time for the one-thirty showing that had been listed in the newspaper. The sea of cars confronting us was daunting. I had never seen the lot so full. John and Margo pulled up next to us as we dithered at the far edge of the lot where a few empty spaces still remained.

"A new three-D movie opened today," said Armando.

"Perhaps that is the reason for the crowd."

"I'll go see what's up," John decided. "You guys park, and I'll be right back." He got out of the car and loped off, moving as easily through the rows of parked cars as a man half his age.

"Is he cute, or what?" Margo cooed as she walked around to the driver's side and took his place.

We wedged our cars into slots, and Margo climbed in with us to wait. In just a few minutes, John returned, only slightly out of breath. "It sold out right in front of me," he reported. "One minute, seats were available, and then pffft! Sold out." He opened the rear door of the Jetta and perched on the seat next to Margo, his long legs folded nearly under his chin.

"It's just amazin' that all these people spend Christmas Day at the movies," Margo marveled. "So much for Norman Rockwell's depictions of Christmas in small-town America."

"Let's not go there," I begged her, still smarting from the events of the previous evening.

John's cell phone rang, and he got out of the car to take the call. "Occupational hazard," Margo explained. "Even when he's not officially on duty, he's on call."

Armando nodded his understanding. "That is true of so many jobs these days, is it not? The TeleCom technicians must always be available by telephone. Instead of freeing us to do other things, I often think all of these devices just keep us on electronic leashes, pulling at us day and night." He changed the subject. "Where can we go that others will not be today?"

"I have a suggestion," said John as he rejoined us. "How about Riverside Park?"

We looked at each other blankly. "Gee," I said, "a brisk walk by the river in twenty-degree weather. Sounds like fun."

"Not fun, maybe, but interesting. A call came into the Hartford Police Department a few minutes ago and was referred to Wethersfield. A jogger at the park spotted a folded-up wheelchair in the brush behind the main building where the path runs right next to the river. The water's high now, because of the rain we had, so it kind of bothered him. Said there was a plastic bag with some men's clothes in it."

"You think it's the chair James O'Halloran took out of the Wadsworth last week," I surmised.

"I more than think it. There's a metal tag on the frame identifying it as property of the Wadsworth Atheneum." He headed for his car. Margo climbed out of the Jetta and joined him.

"We'll go with you," said Armando.

 **Eleven**

Riverside Park lay just north of downtown Hartford on the Connecticut River. As we drove along the entry road, I was struck by the abandoned feel of a summer venue in the dead of winter. Even the dazzling sunshine couldn't mitigate the desolation. Anyone who has had reason to visit a lakeside cottage in December has doubtless had the same lonely sensation. The park, which would be bustling with boaters and ballplayers in a few short months, seemed almost eerie in its emptiness.

Our two-car caravan pulled into the parking lot next to the Jaycees Community Boathouse, an inelegantly named structure that was actually a spacious banquet facility. It, too, sat empty. Only two cars were in the lot, a Hartford police cruiser and a beat-up Chevy. We parked next to the cruiser and joined the uniformed officer who stood talking with a young man wearing wind pants and sneakers. Presumably, he was the jogger who had spotted the wheelchair.

The officer, fortyish and leathery, acknowledged John's introductions with a short nod and got back to the business at hand. "Mr. DiNardi here," he gestured to the jogger, who lifted a hand in greeting, "jogs in this park three times a week. Has a regular route about two miles long. Goes up that path there by the river, runs a mile out, turns around and finishes back here at the boathouse." DiNardi nodded in confirmation. "He hasn't been here in about a week."

"I pulled a hamstring," DiNardi admitted sheepishly.

"He got back to it today. Took his usual route, arrived back here, and sat down on that wall over there to cool out."

"Big Christmas brunch at my in-laws," DiNardi grinned, then quickly sobered. "That's when I saw the chair over there." He pointed to a nearby clump of bushes and underbrush. A collapsible wheelchair and a plastic garbage bag sat on the grass where the sidewalk ended.

We all trooped over to have a look. I was amazed that no barrier existed between the sidewalk and the river. The muddy water slid by swiftly and silently just a few feet from the sidewalk and at nearly the same level. Anyone who was the least bit unsteady on his feet could fall right in. I shivered and kept to the inside of the path. I noticed that Margo did the same thing.

"It wasn't there the last time I jogged here. I would have noticed. But today, there it was, kind of shoved underneath those bushes. It was one of the wheels that caught my eye," Di Nardi reported. "I guess it belongs to the museum. At least, that's what the tag on the frame says. I was glad to see that it didn't belong to a person. I mean, where is he or she?" He glanced at the river, then looked away." Then I opened the bag and saw those clothes. That's when I called the cops." He stopped talking and swallowed hard. I knew how he felt. My stomach wasn't all that happy either.

"When was the last time you ran here?" John asked him.

DiNardi thought about it. "It would have been a week ago Wednesday," he said finally. "I run here on Mondays, Wednesdays and Fridays most weeks."

The next day, Thursday, had been the date of the gala, and on Sunday, Joseph O'Halloran's body had washed up in Wethersfield Cove, which I guessed was about two miles downstream from where we stood. My shivering increased, and Armando put his arm around my shoulders.

After thanking DiNardi and sending him on his way, John and the Hartford officer consulted briefly about the best way to transport the evidence. Together, they maneuvered the chair and the garbage bag into the trunk of the cruiser while Armando shepherded Margo and me back to our cars. We waited for John in the Jetta, the heater going full blast. The day had suddenly turned raw and bleak.

"I don't know about you, but that river slidin' by so fast and quiet just gives me the creeps," said Margo, hugging herself.

"It is a very powerful force. I am sure it has many dark secrets," Armando agreed. He stared at the river, mesmerized.

"Imagine being down here in the dark and the rain," I mused, remembering the night of the gala, "dragging a dead body from the parking lot or wheeling it in that chair and dumping it into the river."

We were silent for a while, contemplating that awful scene. Armando, ever logical, raised the first question. "How could the killer be sure the body would be taken by the river? The main current is quite a distance from the bank, and there is that little inlet just south of here where it could have been snagged on a fallen tree limb." He pointed.

Practical Margo chimed in. "Unless he was very familiar with this place, the killer wouldn't have known about the inlet, and if the water was as high that night as it is now, there would be plenty of current near the bank, as we just saw."

"What I want to know is why James shoved the chair and the clothes under the bushes? Why didn't he pitch them into the river along with his brother's body?" I asked. Both Armando and Margo looked startled. "Well, that's what we're all thinking, isn't it? James was last seen the night of the gala, pushing a plastic garbage bag in a wheelchair out of the Atheneum. Joseph is dead, and James is missing. The evidence all points in the same direction whether we like it or not."

John stood in the parking lot, watching the departing cruiser for a few seconds. Then he beckoned Margo to join him and waved goodbye to Armando and me.

"My lord and master is ready to leave, so I'll be sayin'

goodbye," Margo grumbled, but I noticed that she scrambled to join John. "This has certainly been festive, y'all. Ho ho ho."

We watched them pull away, then followed slowly.

"Where to now?" Armando asked. "Perhaps there is another crime investigation with which the police could use your help."

I glared at his profile, which was hard for me to do. I had always found Armando's face in profile particularly appealing.

"You know perfectly well I had nothing whatsoever to do with this situation. Up until two weeks ago, I hadn't even met these people. Things just happened around me."

Armando smiled to himself. "As they always do, *Cara*," he agreed, patting my knee with resignation.

We drove in silence for a few miles, our minds busy with the ramifications of today's discovery. It seemed all but certain now that James O'Halloran had killed his brother Joseph the night of the UCC gala, whether accidentally or on purpose. His motive for doing so was the remaining mystery, along with his present whereabouts.

From what I knew of the man, which admittedly was very little, I could discern no sufficient motive. Joseph couldn't have been blackmailing James by threatening to tell Mary about Roberta and her son Patrick. Mary already knew about the affair, although James and Joseph may have been unaware that she also knew about James' son born as a result of it. What other deep, dark secret might

Joseph have known about James that would give him leverage over his brother? It was impossible to guess. Only James knew the answer.

That left the question of where James was. The police had sophisticated methods with which to trace missing adults, I knew. Children were tougher, since they did not drive, didn't earn or spend money, and could be more easily controlled and hidden by their abductors. Adults, however, used transportation and required housing and food, all of which had to be purchased. James had disappeared fairly spontaneously more than a week ago. The car he had driven from the UCC to the Wadsworth had been found precisely where he had parked it on the street. His credit cards had not been used, and his bank accounts were intact. He had made one sixty-dollar ATM withdrawal the day before the gala, but since then, nothing. His cell phone had not been used. I thought of the river on what must have been the most desperate night of James' life. Had that despair driven him into the water, too?

I glanced at Armando, who was also deep in thought. Perhaps the full horror of James' actions had overwhelmed him on that terrible night. He had thrown his brother's body into the river and made a half-hearted attempt to conceal the evidence in the underbrush. How far-fetched was it to imagine him following Joseph into the water and swimming out to where the current was the swiftest? It might have seemed fitting to let the river end his misery. It might even have been a relief.

Then how had his car been returned to its parking space on the street outside the Atheneum?

As if reading my thoughts, Armando spoke. "He would not have drowned himself, *Cara*. He would not have done that to his Mary. Whatever he did and wherever he is, his intention has always been to spare her further pain."

I shook my head at my hopelessly romantic Latino. It was exactly the sort of muddle-headed explanation one could expect from a guy whose favorite movie in the world was *An Affair to Remember*. "By abandoning her without even an explanation? By leaving her in a permanent hell of unanswered questions, wondering how she might have helped him, if only he had given her the chance?" I demanded with some heat.

"*Estupido, si?*"

"*Muy estupido*," I agreed, "*y muy macho.*"

Armando shrugged and smiled as he steered us off the highway at the Old Wethersfield exit. It occurred to me that the O'Hallorans' house was less than two miles from here.

"Turn right at the next corner," I said on impulse. "I want to check on Mary."

"Your wish is my command. Perhaps I should acquire one of those hats with the visors that the limousine drivers seem to favor," he said dryly, but I saw the twinkle in his eye.

In just a few minutes, we were pulling into the O'Hallorans' driveway on Wolcott Hill Road. While I hadn't expected a party to be going on under the circumstances, I had hoped that Mary would have a visitor or two to distract her on what had to be a terrible day for her. The little Cape Cod house had an abandoned air, its windows dark, but I climbed out of the car and went to ring the front doorbell. As I listened to it echo through the house, I wondered how she and James had usually spent Christmas, but other than the cruise Mary had been anticipating so eagerly, I could think of no mention of her holiday plans.

I waited until it was obvious that no one was going to answer the door. As I turned to leave, Mary's next door neighbor, the one I had met on my first visit, popped out of her house and trotted across the adjoining lawns to speak to me.

"Hi," she said. "I'm afraid Mary isn't at home. Can I help you with something?"

"Kate Lawrence. We met the other day when I came by to visit Mary," I reminded her. "I work with James at the UCC."

Recognition dawned. "Of course, now I remember. I knew you looked familiar, but things have been a little crazy around here for the past week or so. Mary isn't here," she said again and looked uncomfortable.

"I just wanted to see how she's doing with the holiday and all," I explained. I didn't want to put this nice woman on the spot by prying, but I was eager to know where Mary might be. Surely, she hadn't gone on the intended cruise by herself.

"I guess I'm just being silly," the neighbor decided. She had come out of her house without a coat and hugged herself in the deepening chill. "Mary mentioned you to me and how much she appreciated your concern, so I don't see any reason not to tell you."

"Tell me what?" I asked in sudden alarm.

"The holiday just made all the strain she's been under worse. Everyone was trying so hard to keep her company and see that she had places to go, if she wanted to, and really, all she wanted was to be left alone." I squirmed at her words, knowing I was guilty of just such misguided intentions. "She called me late yesterday evening. She was having palpitations and had trouble getting her breath. My husband and I thought she might be having a heart attack, so we rushed her right to the emergency room at Hartford Hospital."

I was sure my dismay showed on my face. "And was it a heart attack? Is she all right now?"

"No, it wasn't a heart attack. Anxiety, the doctor who examined her said, and it's no wonder. Still, he wanted to do a battery of tests just to be sure about the heart thing, so he had her admitted for overnight observation. They gave her a very mild sedative, and she fell asleep like a stone, poor thing."

"Yes, even temporary oblivion must be most welcome in her situation. I'd probably be drinking myself into a stupor every night, if I were in her shoes." I noticed her shivering and shooed her back inside. "Thanks so much for telling me. I'll call the hospital to see how she's doing."

"They won't tell you anything," the neighbor predicted. "They won't talk to anyone but close relatives. I'll call you when I know what's what," she said and scooted back to her house, where she ducked inside with a final wave.

"Did you find out how Mary is doing?" Armando asked as I settled myself into the passenger seat and fastened my seat belt.

"She's doing lousy, that's how she's doing," I said sadly. "She was admitted to the hospital again last night with a severe anxiety attack."

"I am very sorry to hear that," Armando said, and I knew he meant it.

"Home, James," I said. "I've had just about all the fun I can take for one Christmas."

"How was your Christmas?" I asked Cindy, the technician who answered the phone at Catzablanca on Saturday morning. I had taken my cats there for years and years and was on a first-name basis with most of the staff there.

"Too short," she replied with a sigh. "Yours?"

"Too long," I quipped. "Don't even ask. Listen, I'm coming in with a new cat. Armando rescued her a couple of days ago from a parking lot at the airport. We don't know anything about her, except that she's very timid and has a good appetite. Can you squeeze her into the schedule today for some testing and inoculations?"

"I can't give you an appointment. It's always nuts after a holiday, but you can park her for the day. Dr. DuPont and Dr. Braun are both on today, and between the two of them, they'll figure it out. What's the cat's name?"

"Don't know yet. Spend the day with her, and let me know what you think we should call her," I challenged her.

"You bet. See you soon."

I wrestled a cat carrier out of my bedroom closet under Jasmine's watchful gaze. She immediately vanished underneath my bed.

"It's not for you this time," I told her and took the carrier upstairs, where the new cat still resided in the guest bedroom. After thirty-six hours of incarceration and about six hearty meals, the ginger female had lost a good bit of her timidity. She was savvy enough to recognize a carrier and led Armando and me on a merry chase before I was finally able to nab her. Armando steadied the carrier on end while I stuffed the wriggling creature through the opening, hind legs first, and secured the latches. She bumped the sides in protest, then seemed to accept her fate, however resentfully. Throughout the whole process, she made no sound.

"Poor little thing. I can't imagine what she's already been through this week, and now this. She must be terrified. Does she speak? I've never known such a quiet cat under these circumstances. Usually, they yell bloody murder."

Armando shrugged. "Too frightened, I guess." He toted the carrier downstairs and out to the garage, where he deposited it carefully on the back seat of the Jetta. I closed the car door as quietly as I could manage. We returned to the kitchen for my jacket and purse.

"Emma will be here around eleven to wash glasses and help you move the furniture around. Just follow the diagram the caterer's assistant left the other night."

"The officious little twit?" Armando misquoted me.

"Gnome," I reminded him and kissed his cheek. "Yeah, that one. I'm sorry to stick you with this mess, but I promised Sister Marguerite that I would have that hellacious pile of correspondence answered and ready for her signature on Monday morning, so it's now or never. The vet will call here when the cat's ready to be discharged, and either you or Emma can collect her."

I turned to go, but Armando caught the hem of my jacket. "You will be in that building all alone?"

I wasn't happy about that myself, but I covered my misgivings with what I hoped was a convincing smile. "There are not one, but two, electronically secured doors to get through before you can get into the office, and that's impossible to do unless you have the alarm code. If the silent alarm goes off, the Hartford police will be there, guns drawn, in about three minutes, and there's always 911." My speech was as much to reassure myself as Armando. I gave him a final pat and departed. "Don't forget to give Jasmine some attention," I called over my shoulder.

The ginger cat remained silent on our trip to the veterinary clinic. I spoke quietly to her from time to time, but I doubted that the sound of my voice would reassure her much. I wished she could tell me how she came to be under a car in the airport parking lot, but since that was impossible, I could only surmise that she had escaped from her owners, who would be frantic, in that case. Alternatively, she had been dumped by owners who no longer wanted her. Neither scenario was uplifting. I could only deal with things as they were.

Cindy, Jana and Beth were all on duty when I arrived at Catzablanca, and they crowded around to coo at the new kitty. "She's not a kitten, but she's not very old either," Jana pronounced, and the others concurred.

"I don't even know if she's been spayed," I admitted. "In fact, I know absolutely nothing about her."

"We'll scan her to see if she's been microchipped, in which case we can probably get her back to her owners. Otherwise, are you willing to adopt her?" Cindy asked, already knowing what my answer would be.

"If she's negative for feline leukemia, yes. Jasmine can't be exposed to that, since we stopped inoculating her against it a couple of years ago because of her age. So if this cat is positive, we'll have to find another home for her, but I'll take financial responsibility, of course. Check her out, and give Armando a call. He's at the house, or you can call me with the results of her blood test." I gave them my phone number at the UCC. "I'll talk to you later."

It broke my heart to abandon the stray one more time, but I figured she didn't know me well enough yet to care much, and she needed to be examined. I knew that she couldn't be in better hands. The technicians and Drs.

DuPont and Braun would be very kind to her.

I pulled into the lot at the UCC and parked as close to the building as I could. Dark clouds had rolled in, and snow threatened once again. More likely, it would be rain, since the temperature was in the high thirties. I hoped Mother Nature would get it over with and give us a decent day tomorrow for the wedding. Before I let myself in with the coded key fob I had been issued, which was readable by the scanner outside the back door, I made sure I had the alarm code in my hand. After opening the door, I would have only thirty seconds in which to deactivate the alarm, or the police would be alerted to a possible break-in.

I entered the building and deactivated the alarm without incident. The floors had been freshly mopped, I noted, and I wiped my feet carefully on the interior doormat. Apparently, I wasn't the only one working on the day after Christmas. I waved my key fob at the second scanner just outside the main office door, and that lock was released, as well. I went in and closed the door firmly behind me, then flipped the light switch on the wall. The overhead lights went on throughout the main level. The building was strangely silent after the bustle of the last week, but I told myself that was a good thing. Without colleagues around to distract me, I could finish my work and get home more quickly.

As I passed the little kitchen area, I knew I had been correct to assume that lunch wouldn't be a problem. After my first day at the UCC, I had realized that I was going to have to spend a lot of my time there resisting temptation if

I wanted to avoid changing sizes. The staff might be accustomed to long hours and slim paychecks, but none of them would ever go hungry. On any given morning, half of the people who worked in the building arrived bearing goodies, whether leftovers from home or baked especially for everyone at work to share. Any meeting held after 11:00 a.m. was reason enough to order in pizza, and there was always plenty to spare. I had brown-bagged my lunch the first day and then realized it would be totally unnecessary. Thereafter, I had just contributed to the perpetual buffet, adding fresh fruit, carrots and celery to the mix.

The Christmas season only accelerated the food frenzy. The number and variety of the daily offerings were astounding. I became accustomed to talking with people, either on the phone or in person, whose mouths were full. This morning, breads, pies, cookies and doughnuts from last week still covered every available surface and spilled over into the conference room.

I shook my head and proceeded to my desk, where the mound of papers appeared twice the size it had been when I last saw it. How that was possible, I had no idea, but the sooner I tackled it, the better. I clicked on the little radio Mary Alice kept at her desk for company and was soon totally engrossed.

Without distractions, I was able to finalize a good deal of the post-gala correspondence and other paperwork that Sister Marguerite and Mary Alice would need in the weeks ahead. My concentration on my task was such that I was surprised to lift my head and see that it was already two o'clock. I rose creakily from my chair and stretched. My best guess was that I had another hour or so of work ahead of me, but my joints needed some exercise. I decided to take a quick walk around the block to clear my head.

After setting the security alarm, I let myself out the back door with just my key chain in my pocket. Best not to carry a handbag in this neighborhood, Shirley had often reminded me in her kindly but realistic way. I strolled out to Asylum Avenue and turned right. Traffic was relatively light on the weekend, but there was no point in having to cross a lot of streets. Dark clouds hovered in the sky overhead, but my jacket was waterproof and had a hood, so they didn't bother me. The cold, clear air felt delicious, and I had plenty to think about. I picked up my pace to get the blood flowing and stuck my hands in my pockets as I considered the events of the past few days and those to come tomorrow.

In about a quarter of a mile, I turned right onto Asylum Place, which took me downhill to Farmington Avenue, and turned right again. After looking at the rear of the Cathedral for so many days, it was interesting to get a good look at it from the front. I paused at the bottom of the steps and craned my neck upward. The back of the structure was very utilitarian, giving the place the look of a fortress, but from the front it was very impressive. The massive wreath suspended at the entrance softened the look still further. I was sure that the Christmas Eve and Christmas Day services had been packed, but now, the

Cathedral looked deserted. Well, tomorrow was Sunday, and things would be back to normal.

I walked on, enjoying the exercise and the fresh air after being confined for several hours. I turned right onto Sigourney Street, which would take me back to Asylum and the UCC office. As I rounded the corner, the clouds that I had noticed earlier opened up, and it began to rain, first a sprinkle, then in earnest. I pulled the hood of my jacket up over my head and made a run for it, which amounted to a fairly sedate trot. It wouldn't do to hit an icy patch and sprain an ankle.

I reached the back door and fumbled in my pocket for the key fob that would gain me admittance. I waved it in front of the scanner and yanked open the door. That's when I remembered the code I would need to deactivate the alarm, or rather, I didn't remember it. I stood gaping at the alarm, trying to think what to do. Call the police and tell them I was an idiot? Just wait for them to show up? My heart raced. Then I noticed that the light on the alarm box, which should have been red, was green. That meant the alarm had already been deactivated, or had I not correctly set it when I left the building for my walk? I struggled to remember, but I could not actually visualize the light turning red before I'd let myself out the door. No doubt I'd done it wrong, but thank goodness no harm had been done. There were still the two electronic locks securing the office from unwanted intrusion.

My heart slowed as I climbed the short staircase to the office entrance, but not for long. On the freshly mopped floor I had noticed earlier, there was now a trail of wet, slightly muddy footprints leading directly to the interior door. I paused, key fob in hand, then laughed at my own foolishness. Of course. Another member of the staff had come into the office while I was out enjoying my walk. That explained the footprints and the fact that the alarm had been deactivated. The question was, who would be keeping me company?

I let myself in. The lights were still on, as I had left them. "Hello!" I called loudly, not wanting to frighten any other staff member who might also think he or she was in the building alone. "It's Kate Lawrence. Anybody home?" Silence. I traversed the short hall by the conference room and stood at the bottom of the stairs. "Hello?" I called again. "It's just me, Kate Lawrence. Who else is here toiling away on a Saturday?" Still no answer. I climbed the first few steps to the second floor before I noticed that no lights were on upstairs. "Anybody there?" I called more doubtfully, but again, there was no response. I stopped in my tracks as the hairs on the back of my neck prickled atavistically.

Enlightenment washed over me. I wasn't alone in the building. Of that, I was quite certain. I was equally sure that the person who had joined me didn't want his presence known—but I did know. What's more, I knew who he was.

Twelve

The stairs leading to the attic were wide and sturdy, no doubt constructed to facilitate the movement of heavy computer equipment up and down them. Because the original rickety steps had been replaced just a few years ago when the UCC moved in, they hadn't been used all that much and were relatively clean. The wet imprints of a man's hard-soled dress shoes stood out clearly on the first few steps.

I flipped the lights on and climbed slowly to the top, where I sat and looked around. It all looked as it had on my first visit, including the tarp-draped stack of large cartons in the far corner. It was this sad little structure that I addressed.

"James," I said in a conversational tone, "it's Kate Lawrence, Mary Alice's replacement during her maternity leave. We met at the planning meetings for the gala. My partner Charlene sold you and Mary your house in Wethersfield. Do you remember?"

I stopped talking and listened. The only sound was that of the light rain, mixed with a little sleet now, pattering on the roof and windows.

"Mary is safe, James. Your neighbor is keeping an eye on her, but she's completely distraught. She had an anxiety attack on Christmas Eve and had to be admitted to Hartford Hospital overnight. She simply cannot live with the idea that you may have abandoned her."

I paused again to allow my words to sink in. "Whatever went on between you and your brother can be sorted out. Mary loves you so much, James. She can forgive you anything if only she knows that you're alive and love her, too. At the moment, she doesn't know that. You need to tell her. It's time. It's past time."

A brisk wind had blown up. It moaned eerily through the cracks and crevices and rattled a window somewhere behind me. I shivered and pulled my jacket sleeves down over my hands. An almost imperceptible rustling emanated from the pile in the corner. The tarpaulin was thrown back, and James struggled wearily to his feet. He stood, swaying a little in his wet raincoat and rumpled suit, looking like one of the homeless men I had seen at the food pantry at the Cathedral. His unshaven face was haggard, his eyes bleak. Slowly, he took the dozen or so paces necessary to reach me and sank down next to me on the top step.

"Tell me about Mary," he rasped. I was pretty sure those were the first words he had spoken in a week.

"I will," I promised, "but first, we need to get you some food. Come downstairs where it's warmer. There's food all over the place down there." As I heard myself say it, I realized that James must have been living off the largesse of his colleagues all week. "You're wet. I'll heat something up for you in the microwave," I amended and rose to my feet.

James grabbed my arm. Even through my jacket, I could feel how cold his hand was. "Mary," he repeated loudly. "I have to know that she's all right. Please." I resumed my seat and twisted sideways to look him full in the face.

"She's safe, James, as I told you, but this has been the worst week of her life. She needs to hear from you. Couldn't you at least have called her?"

"Couldn't risk it," he said, his voice becoming a little clearer with use. "They can trace anything these days, and if they thought she knew where I was, they would have made her life miserable."

"Her life *has* been miserable, James. Can you even imagine how frightened and worried she's been, still is, not knowing if you're dead or alive? Have you been here the whole time since last Thursday night, holed up in this freezing attic?"

"I couldn't think where else to go that they wouldn't find me. I needed time to think, to figure out what to do. It wasn't so bad. I had a stadium blanket from my car and my coat. I went to the Cathedral sometimes. That's where I was now. I didn't know you'd be coming back. At night I went downstairs and made hot coffee. It wasn't easy in the dark, but it doesn't matter about me. The only thing that matters is Mary."

I searched his face. "Then how could you do this to her, James?"

He jumped to his feet and paced wildly between the staircase and the server housing. "I had no choice! There was nothing else I could do, can't you understand? I had no choice about any of it, not from the very beginning nearly twenty years ago. I just paid and paid and paid, anything to keep Mary from being hurt."

The pieces of his personal dilemma began to sort themselves into a tragic picture in my mind. "Do you mean Roberta and Patrick, James? Is that what you so desperately didn't want Mary to know? Well, you can let go of that now. Mary knows, and she loves you anyway. Her love is unconditional, James. So you can come out of hiding and go home and let her help you through this, whatever it is." I spoke firmly in an attempt to penetrate his agitation and got to my feet. He stared at me, thunderstruck. "Now come downstairs with me and call your wife." I started down the stairs. Without another word, and to my huge relief, James followed me.

Back on the first floor, James sat quietly at the reception desk while I foraged for something more nourishing than the ubiquitous pastries. Now that he had been discovered, he seemed strangely at peace. For the moment, it appeared to be enough to be surrounded by

warmth and light and to have contact with another human
being.

I tried to imagine what it must have been like, hiding
like an animal in the attic day after day and coming out to
find food only in the dark. He would have had to be silent
and nearly motionless after the accounting and
development staff arrived on the second floor around nine
in the morning and stay that way until the group residence
staff left the building between seven and eight in the
evening. Even on the weekend, he would have had to be
alert, since every staff member had the security alarm code
and a key to the building, and they often came in at odd
hours to catch up on paperwork.

I settled on a can of chicken noodle soup from the stash
Mary Alice kept in her desk drawer. While it heated in the
microwave, I fought the urge to call Mary. I knew I should
be notifying the police, but which police? The Hartford
police, since the death had occurred there, or the
Wethersfield police, since the body had been discovered
there? Well, they could all wait half an hour until James
got himself a bit more together, I decided.

I set a steaming bowl of soup in front of him. The
napkin and spoon I put down beside it prompted a small
smile.

"Nice," he said, "a woman's touch." His face contorted
as he struggled with the powerful emotions he had kept
bottled up for more than a week now. My heart went out
to him, and I busied myself at the sink to give him time to

regroup. When I turned back, he was spooning soup into his mouth steadily, his hand trembling only a little.

When he finished his meal, he placed the spoon neatly in the empty bowl and used the napkin. We regarded one another across the empty reception area. "Now what?" he asked, and I had to admit I hadn't a clue. "I did it, of course. I killed my brother Joseph. It was an accident, but I don't think anyone will believe that, especially since I ran away."

"I believe it," I told him honestly. Again, the briefest of smiles.

"Thank you. I appreciate knowing that. I've had a lot of time to think about it. I had endured Joseph's cadging and mooching, his endless requests for money and his failed business schemes, for years. Mary and I both had. After that, there was the terrible situation with Roberta, and then Patrick came along." He dropped his head into his hands.

"I don't need to know," I hastened to interject. "It's between you and Mary."

"The police," he added. "Mustn't forget about them. I've screwed up in the past, God knows, but this time, God himself can't help me."

I decided my opinion on that subject wouldn't do anything to reassure James and kept quiet.

"Joseph lived in California, not far from Roberta. They were actually both members of the local chapter of the National Society of Certified Public Accountants and had met once or twice at functions. I needed a way to get money to Roberta that Mary wouldn't question, so I took Joseph into my confidence." His face twisted at his folly. "Major mistake number two. At first, he seemed to do as I asked, although I had my doubts that everything I sent actually made it to Roberta for Patrick's care. Then one year, when I made my annual trip out west and stopped by to visit my son, Joseph answered the door."

"He had married Roberta," I said unnecessarily, since we both already knew that to be true.

"How did you know?"

"The police learned it during the missing persons investigation, which is what this started out to be."

He nodded. "Of course, I forgot about that. All those years of trying to keep my hideous blunders under wraps, and now the whole world knows that I'm not only a fool but a murderer," he summed up bleakly.

"You said it was an accident," I protested. "That doesn't sound like murder to me."

"I covered it up, or at least, I tried to. I took my dead brother's body out of a public place in full view of about a dozen witnesses and threw it in the river. I had some crazy idea that if it stayed in the water long enough, it would be so decomposed that the authorities would believe it was me, and Mary could at least collect my life insurance. I just had to stay out of the way, disappear from her life. How is that even possible?" he said in obvious bewilderment. "I'm a financial professional. That was the thinking of a madman."

"Very likely," I pointed out. "The plea of temporary insanity exists for a reason, James."

He turned that over in his mind. "I don't even remember exactly how it happened. One minute, I was in the Education Office at the Wadsworth, where the caterer's staff kept the replenishment hors d'oeuvres and a big container of champagne punch. I was laying out the pieces of my Santa Claus suit. The next minute, there was Joseph, standing right in front of me, threatening to tell Mary everything if I didn't give him yet more money, but there *wasn't* any more money. He and Roberta had bled me dry. I took a loan against what was left of my retirement fund to give Mary one last trip, one good memory, before I confessed everything to her. I just had to acknowledge my son, you see. I couldn't stand not to do that any longer. But Joseph kept pushing, kept insisting. Mary was due any minute. I had to make him stop talking, just stop talking." His expression turned fierce at the memory, then crumbled.

"We struggled. I hit him, and he fell. All I remember is bolting out of there. I wanted to find Mary before Joseph did, but I missed her in the crowd. I went back into the office to confront Joseph once and for all. That's when I found him slumped over the edge of the caterer's vat, face down in the punch. I dragged him out, but it was too late. He must have been unconscious when he went down, and he drowned." He pulled his gaze away from the window and stared at me, his face a mixture of horror and incredulity. "He drowned in a goddamned vat of Christmas punch."

Having gotten it all out, he sank back in the chair, his eyes empty and his hands limp on the desk before him. Clearly, it was time for me to take action, but what should I do? So I did what I usually do when I need a clearer head than my own. I waited for James to drag himself into the men's room, and I called Margo.

"Hey, there, Sugar. All ready for the big weddin' tomorrow? John and I will be there to help you cope."

It was symptomatic of my current state of mind that I had forgotten about the wedding for the moment. "Hard as it may be to believe, the wedding is the last thing on my mind at the moment," I told her. "Is John home?"

"He came in from his racquetball game about an hour ago. He's upstairs as we speak getting' all spiffed up to take his gorgeous wife out to dinner and a movie, the one we didn't get to see yesterday." She giggled in anticipation.

"I'm afraid you might not be seeing it tonight either. Put John on an extension, will you? I need him to hear this, too."

Margo heard the urgency in my voice and snapped to attention. "You bet, Hon," was all she said. Within seconds, the three of us were connected, and I launched into a condensed version of today's events. James returned to his seat and sat quietly until I hung up the phone.

"Now what?" he asked again. "Are the police coming here, or do I turn myself in? More importantly, who's going to be with Mary while all of this is happening?"

"You are," I told him and outlined the plan that Margo, John and I had concocted. As he listened, his eyes filled alternately with hope, regret, and finally anguish.

"You are all being so kind to me," he choked. "It's overwhelming. You don't even know me. I hardly know myself anymore. This whole thing feels as if it's happening to someone else." He wiped the welling tears from his eyes roughly.

"You haven't been yourself, James. That's what I've been trying to tell you. By the way," I added, realizing why I hadn't quite recognized him during the music rehearsal at the Cathedral. "What happened to your eyeglasses?"

He reached into the pocket of his rumpled raincoat and produced a pair of ruined spectacles. One lens was shattered, and an earpiece was missing. "I don't even remember where this happened," he said. He put them back in his pocket. "Can we go now? I want to get myself cleaned up a little before Mary sees me."

I smiled inwardly at this reassertion of personal pride. It wasn't much, but it was a start.

On the way to Hubbard Plaza in Rocky Hill, just south of Wethersfield, we passed Catzablanca, which is when I remembered the ginger cat. I pulled into the hotel parking lot and called the vet's office.

"Not to worry," Cindy assured me. "When we couldn't reach you at work, I called the house. Armando collected Gracie about half an hour ago. She's fine, by the way. No feline leukemia."

"That's great news," I told her. "Gracie?"

"Ditzy little blonde, you know, like George Burns' wife, Gracie Allen. She's kind of timid at first, but I think she's going to be a real charmer, just the thing to give Jasmine a new interest in life."

"Okay, Gracie it is," I agreed and promised to make another appointment soon.

Hubbard Plaza is one of the nicer conference facilities outside Hartford's city limits. It offers a formal hotel with all the amenities, including a concierge and room service, in one building and extended-stay suites with kitchenettes and exterior entrances in several smaller facilities on the property. It was the latter that John and Margo had suggested for what I had in mind.

We arrived in the parking lot within minutes of each other. John pulled up next to my Jetta, which I'd parked beneath a lamppost to be clearly visible. Although it was not yet five o'clock, dark had descended.

John got out of his car, and James got out of my car to join him. "We're going to suite fourteen in building three," John said to me, pointing to the structure at the far right of the lot. "Margo will be right along. Just knock." I gave James what I hoped was an encouraging smile, and together, the two men walked across the lot and disappeared inside.

I turned on the all-news station for company but switched off the radio after the first two stories of brutality and senseless mayhem, preferring my own thoughts to the commentator's relentless yammering. I could not bear to think about the errand Margo had bravely undertaken and what Mary's reaction to the news of her husband's discovery must have been. Joy? Anger? Stoic acceptance, perhaps, after all that she had already endured and had yet to face. What would I do if it were Armando in that room with John right now?

Before I arrived at any conclusions, Margo's elegant little coupe slid into the space next to me on the other side. The imagery of being safely bracketed by Harknesses comforted me. She climbed out and came around to where I still sat behind the wheel, leaving Mary in her car's passenger seat.

"How did it go?" I asked in a low voice.

"I'm not really sure," she answered with her usual candor. "No hysterics, no hissy fit. Not much reaction at all, come to think of it, just this eerie calm after I told her what had happened and where we were goin'. It was almost as if she had expected this. They would have had to put me in a straitjacket in her place, but she just excused herself and went upstairs to put her husband's shavin' kit and some clean clothes in a suitcase. No muss, no fuss, and distinctly weird."

I got out of the car and beeped it locked. "She's in shock. Come on, let's get this over with."

A minute later, John answered our knock at the door of suite fourteen. "He's in here, Mrs. O'Halloran. He's a little worse for wear, but he's okay. His glasses are broken, and he hasn't had access to a razor in more than a week, but he's all right and very anxious to see you."

Margo and I stood behind Mary, ready to catch her if she collapsed, but her composure held. "I brought him some things I knew he would need," she said and held out the little suitcase she had brought with her. Her eyes searched the room beyond John, and he stepped aside.

James stood in the center of the room, still wet from a shower. He wore a terrycloth robe, thoughtfully provided by the hotel. His eyes were riveted on Mary where she stood at the door.

John took the suitcase she held out and put it on the end of the bed. "There's no point in trying to deal with the legalities tonight, so James has agreed to turn himself in to the Wethersfield police at ten o'clock tomorrow morning. There will be an officer parked outside this building tonight in an unmarked car." He stopped talking, since it was clear that neither James nor Mary was listening to him. He looked at us and shrugged.

Margo gave Mary a little push, and she stumbled into the room. Her eyes never left her husband as she ran to him and grabbed him by both shoulders. John looked a little alarmed, but Margo shook her head at him.

"You stupid son of a bitch," Mary said. Then she stood on tiptoe and hugged him fiercely.

We backed out of the room, and John pulled the door

shut. We exchanged satisfied smiles as the promised police officer pulled up beside us to consult briefly with John. He took up his position in the first row of parking spaces and cut the engine of his unmarked vehicle.

"Poor guy," Margo sympathized. "He has to sit there all night? What does he do when, uh, he has to use the facilities?"

"They're equipped to deal with that," John told her without elaborating. "Anyway, he'll only be there for four hours. The duty will rotate among several officers."

"What will happen to James, John? In his own mind, he's responsible for his brother's death, but it was an accident, a freak accident."

John looked at me in the lamplight as if considering my ability to hear what he was about to say. "That part isn't really the problem," he said finally, "or at least, it wouldn't have been if he'd busted out of that room at the Wadsworth yelling for help when he found his brother. No one in his right mind would have believed a man would deliberately try to drown someone in a vat of punch." He shook his head. "No, it was what he did next that will turn a jury against him, if it comes to that."

"You mean, trying to cover it up?"

John ticked off points on his fingers. "He fished his brother's body out of the punch and dressed it in a Santa suit. Then he put him in a garbage bag and wheeled the body out of the museum. He drove to the boat launch, tipped Joseph into the river, and carefully put his car back exactly where he had originally parked it. Finally, he hiked all the way across town to the UCC and made himself invisible for more than a week. He didn't come to his senses the next day and call somebody. He laid low for eight days, and who knows how much longer he would have been there if you hadn't figured it out."

John's matter-of-fact summation made my blood run cold. "He wanted people to think it was he who had died so his wife could collect on his life insurance," I pointed out in James' defense.

"That was never going to work," John said in disgust. "There are all kinds of physical evidence used to identify a body, like dental records, DNA, traces of medications. Besides, if he cared so much about his wife, did he consider how she would feel having to view the remains? She was pretty lucky Joseph had been in the water only three days when she saw him. After a week, they get … well." He thought better of supplying details.

"So it's not so much Joseph's death but the cover up that's got James in over his head?" My words replayed in my mind. I clapped a hand over my mouth but couldn't contain an involuntary giggle at my unfortunate metaphor. Margo picked up on it immediately.

"Out of his depth?" she offered and snorted.

"Going down for the third time?" I choked, and we both howled.

"You two are sick," was John's only comment.

"You're right, we're bad people," Margo said. We pulled ourselves together. "Now, I believe someone promised me dinner and a movie." She patted her husband's backside discreetly. I couldn't see in the dim light, but I was sure John was blushing. "What are you and your fella gettin' up to tonight, Sugar?"

I had a sudden vision of Armando up to his elbows in a sinkful of dirty glassware while hungry cats yowled around his ankles.

"Oh my God, I've got to get home," I blurted in a panic. I headed for my car at a trot. "Armando and Emma have been coping with the whole wedding thing by themselves all day, not to mention the new cat."

"New cat?" Margo called after me.

"Gracie, you'll meet her tomorrow. See you then. You guys are the best."

I started the car and tore out of the lot at an imprudent rate of speed, considering that two of Wethersfield's finest were watching me. At the first light, I checked my watch. Nearly six o'clock, and I had planned to be home to help in mid-afternoon. Well, at least I had a great excuse.

I pulled into the garage and ran up the stairs to the kitchen door. When I opened it, I fully expected to find pandemonium, but all was quiet. The kitchen was in surprisingly good order, and something appetizing simmered on the stove. I followed the smell of wood smoke into the living room, where logs blazed cheerfully in the fireplace. Armando and Emma sat companionably on the sofa, enjoying a glass of wine. They looked up when I came in and stopped dead in my tracks.

"Hi, Momma. We didn't hear you," Emma stated the obvious, but I was too stunned to respond. I very nearly

didn't recognize my own home. In the few hours I had
been gone, the space before me had been transformed from
a run-of-the-mill dining-living room into an elegant
holiday setting for a wedding. The furniture had been
moved to the walls to open up the space. Damask-draped
tables formed a buffet on which crystal and silver gleamed.
A small side table stood at the ready for the wedding cake.

What had been the pass-through from kitchen to
dining room was now a fully stocked wet bar. Tasteful
arrangements of white roses and baby's breath mixed with
seasonal greenery now complemented the Christmas tree
and a few other decorations that had been allowed to
remain. A bridal garland on the mantel indicated where
the ceremony would take place, and short rows of satin-
padded folding chairs were arranged down the center of
the room in front of the mantel. Very simply, the place was
drop-dead gorgeous.

"How did you do this? Did the caterer's staff help?"

Emma gave Armando a thumbs-up. "Oh, they came by
around noon and dropped off some glasses and silverware
and stuff, and the florist delivered a lot of roses, but we
pulled it all together. So you like it?"

"Like it? I love it! I can't believe this is our house. Jeff
and Donna will be absolutely thrilled. I think you two
should go into the catering business yourselves." I crossed
to where they sat and gave each of them a big hug. "I'm so
sorry I got held up, but wait until you hear what
happened."

Armando put a glass of wine into my hand and pushed

me gently into the big easy chair opposite the sofa. After just a few sentences, they were hanging on my every word, their eyes round.

"Wow," was Emma's succinct reaction when I finally wound down.

Armando's eyes danced as he gazed at me across the room. "So once again, Wethersfield's answer to Jessica Fletcher has solved the crime," he joked gently. "I am sure the police are grateful for your assistance, as they have been in the past." Despite his teasing words, I could hear the pride in his voice.

"Depends on who you ask," I replied. "I don't think that young man sitting in the Hubbard Plaza parking lot for the next several hours is all that happy with me. Anyway, I'm starving. Emma, are you staying to share whatever it is on the stove that smells so good?"

She drained her glass and jumped to her feet. After the day she had put in, I admired her energy. "No can do, Momma, sorry." She headed for the kitchen.

"Big plans for the evening?" Armando twitted her. I knew he was as happy as I was to see her regaining her energy and spirit. She stuck her head back into the room as she shrugged into her coat.

"As a matter of fact, I do," she retorted. "I've been invited to a party, and I'm going, so there." She caught my eye and winked. "Don't worry, Momma. I'm back."

"I can see that. Have a good time."

"I intend to," she assured me. "See you guys tomorrow," and she was gone.

Thirteen

"Are you excited?" I asked Jeff on the phone the next morning.

"Right at the moment, I don't know what I am, Aunt Kate. I'm worried about Donna. If I'm interpreting the awful noises coming from the bathroom correctly, she's in there throwing up."

"Perfectly normal," I assured him. "I'm sure it's just a thumping good case of the jitters combined with morning sickness. Surely this isn't a new thing."

"If she's been having this kind of morning sickness, she's done a great job of keeping it a secret from me," Jeff said."

"Well, give her a couple of Saltines when this bout passes, and tell her everything here is under control," I told him, but I neglected to mention that I had my fingers crossed.

To tell the truth, I wasn't feeling all that perky myself. The events of the past week had really taken their toll on me, physically and emotionally, and I still had this wedding to get through. When the Ghost of Christmas

Past came to haunt me in years to come, I hoped he wouldn't choose this one for me to revisit.

I poured a cup of coffee and took it upstairs to Armando. He lay on his back, covers pulled neatly over his chest, snoring gently. Gracie looked up from where she was nestled in the crook of his arm.

"Good morning," I said to her. She squinted her amber eyes at me. "If you've picked him out as your person, that's fine, but you should know that he's kind of tough to get up in the morning."

Her eyelids drooped shut, and she resumed her nap. *Great, they're a perfect match.* I plunked the mug down on the bedside table.

"Wake up, Sleepyhead. Salma Hayek is at the front door. She says she's here to make wild, passionate love to you."

A smile curled Armando's lips. Just as I thought, he was faking. Too late, I tried to dodge out of his reach. He caught me by the wrist and pulled me down next to him. Gracie lumped off in disgust, and I took her place, my head on Armando's shoulder.

"What time is it?" he asked, still without opening his eyes.

"Ten o'clock. Emma will be back with Michael and Sheila and Sheila's mother in about an hour, and the caterer will be here at noon."

"So we have a whole hour to ourselves, do we not?"

I recognized that tone. "Not a chance," I told him. "If Margo and John show up early and catch us canoodling,

I'll never hear the end of it." I struggled to an upright position and slid off the bed. "John's at the police station right now with James," I added for good measure.

Armando sat up and reached for his coffee. "Do not dwell on it, *Cara*. You have done everything you possibly can for these people, and now it is out of your hands. It will be what it will be. Today is for happier thoughts."

He was right, of course.

"By the way, where did you put my gray suit? I did not see it in my closet last night."

I clapped both hands to my head. In all the confusion yesterday, I had completely forgotten to collect his suit from the dry cleaner. Armando shrugged, unperturbed.

"So I guess I will be wearing something else today, is that what you are telling me?"

"I'm so sorry," I apologized before darting from the room to answer the phone, which was ringing off the hook in the kitchen. "Wedding Central," I answered with manufactured cheer. The day was off and running, and so was I.

At eleven o'clock almost to the minute, Emma let herself in the front door. Sheila was right behind her with her mother. Sheila herself was a vision of understated elegance in a shell-pink, Chanel-style suit and low-heeled pumps. Her stylish brunette bob framed a face that simultaneously radiated embarrassment and resignation. Emma waggled her eyebrows at me meaningfully, and I understood Sheila's discomfiture immediately.

"I don't think you've ever met Sheila's mother, have

you, Momma? Grandma Mitzi, this is Joey's and my mom, Kate Lawrence."

"Hi, there, Sheila, come on in. Mitzi, welcome. It's a pleasure to meet you. I've heard so much about you." *None of it good,* I added silently. In stark contrast to her daughter, Mitzi had gaga old lady written all over her from her flowered straw hat, circa 1959, to the wrinkled stockings that sagged around her skinny ankles. The rest of her was covered by a girlish dress with a full skirt, two sizes too big for her, in a violent shade of yellow. It hurt to look at her.

"Pleased to meetcha, I'm sure," she said, extending a wizened claw tipped with red acrylic nails. "I don't understand why we're here. Who's getting married this time?" Bright lipstick that matched her frightening nails wandered uncertainly across her mouth.

"I've told you, Mom. Michael's nephew Jeff is marrying his fiancée Donna this afternoon." She ushered her mother firmly down the hall to the living room.

"Oh, I know Michael, all right. He's that bigshot you're married to now, drove us over here from the hotel. Where'd he get to?"

I had been asking myself the very same thing.

"He's parking the car down the street," Emma explained. "We didn't want to block the driveway, or the caterer won't be able to get in."

Oh, good Lord, I had forgotten all about the parking situation. Between the caterer and the sixty invited guests, there could be upwards of forty vehicles jockeying for position on The Birches' quiet streets by two o'clock. Would that number of cars even be tolerated by the condominium association? I foresaw a nasty-gram from the property management company in my future.

Oh, well, too late now, I thought, *Still, the caterer has to be able to get in and out*. I grabbed Emma and begged for her help. "I'm on it," she said and vanished back outside to keep traffic away from the driveway. "Hi, Mary," she greeted my next-door neighbor on the way out, and I cringed anew. On her best day, Mary was a loose cannon. The idea of her in the same room with Grandma Mitzi during a solemn, formal occasion was downright alarming.

"What's cookin', Snookums?" Mary greeted me, her eyes bright behind her thick spectacles. "Where's your ex? I'm dying to get a squint at him."

"Right behind you," I informed her sourly. "Come on in, Michael, and join the party."

He did, grinning from ear to ear, and introduced himself to Mary. Michael's easygoing nature and genuine niceness had always been attractive to the ladies, and Mary was no exception. She goggled at him happily.

"So where's the new wife?" she demanded after names had been exchanged. "I want to get a look at her, too."

"Sure thing," Michael agreed affably. He gave me a peck on the cheek and a wink. "Come along with me, and I'll introduce you. You didn't lock Sheila in the basement like you did the last time, did you, Kate?" He took Mary's arm and ushered her down the hallway. "Thanks again,

Kate. The house looks great," he said over his shoulder. I shook my head and remembered once again how much I liked Michael. We made much better friends than we had spouses.

Promptly at noon, the caterer's trucks pulled into the driveway. They were followed closely by Margo. "What's familiar about these guys?" she wondered aloud. She tapped her chin with a beautifully manicured finger.

"They all pretty much look alike in those white smocks, don't they?" I yanked her into the kitchen for a private conference. "Where's John? How did it go at the station?"

"He'll be along soon, Sugar. As far as I know, it all went accordin' to plan. James showed up, and Mary was with him. They did their thing, but there's a lot of paperwork, statements to be taken and so forth. It bein' Sunday, it's tough to get a magistrate on board, so that takes more time. Then they have to find a bail bondsman. You know how it goes."

I didn't, but I was willing to take her word for it. Margo went to join the others in the living room and play hostess for me. At that moment, Emma opened the door between the kitchen and the garage. A procession of white-coated catering staff filed in, burdened with food and equipment. For several minutes, it was pandemonium. Then everything fell smoothly into place, and the crew became a team of seasoned professionals.

Bringing up the rear was the big boss himself. *At last, I get to meet the big cheese,* I thought, and found myself face to face with Henry Kozlowski.

"Henri? Is it really you?" I beamed at him, remembering how he had created the spectacular diversion on the fly at the Wadsworth gala when James went missing. He had absolutely saved the evening.

"Never fear, *ma petite*, Henri is here," he said in an affected French accent reminiscent of old war movies. Then he snapped his gum and gave me a big squeeze. "How's the fundraising biz, Sweetie?" His staff went calmly about their business, unaware of my connection to the nearly disastrous gala.

"I never realized that East Hartford Catering was you. My ex-husband made all the arrangements."

"That would be the big, good-looking one, right?" he said wistfully. "Why is it that all the really great men have wives?" He sighed. "Oh, well. Not to worry, Sweetie. This meal is to die for."

"Now I know everything will be fine," I grinned at him and went to get Armando out of the shower and moving in the right direction.

I found him sitting on the end of his bed, buttoning a white dress shirt. In addition to the shirt, he wore black silk shorts and black socks. Armando's casual, South American relationship with time had always irritated me, and I struggled to keep my temper. "Hurry up, Handsome. The house is filling up with people. I need you downstairs being charming," I pleaded.

He pointed to a pile of clothes on the floor in front of his closet. Gracie lay snugly on top, her tail curled over her nose. "Nothing fits," he said sadly. "I cannot button any of those things because I am becoming, how do you call it, piggy."

"Porky," I corrected him without thinking, then bit my lip. "Don't be silly. You're not getting fat. You've put on a few pounds, but I happen to like your tummy. So pick something out of that pile, and get downstairs quick. Just leave the jacket open."

He remained motionless. "I am becoming a fat old man," he insisted. I gritted my teeth.

"Honey, you're going to be the best-looking man in the room, as usual. So please, please get moving. You can start your midlife crisis tomorrow, I promise. Don't forget to shut Gracie up in here when you come downstairs."

Throughout our conversation, the doorbell had bonged almost continuously as Jeff and Donna's young friends began arriving. I peeked out an upstairs window to assess the parking situation and was surprised to see Joey greeting the arriving guests. He was directing them to available parking spaces on side streets, which were rapidly filling up. I was filled with gratitude, but as I watched my handsome, capable son, I was also overcome with an awareness of the passage of time. My quirky little nephew Jeff was getting married today, Donna was expecting their child, and my own baby boy was outside my house looking more mature and assured than he could possibly be old enough to be.

I had to remind myself that Joey had routinely managed a seventy-three-foot rig in all kinds of traffic and weather for a couple of years now, and it wasn't only he who had grown up while I wasn't paying attention. His little sister had just had her heart broken, but she was downstairs with a smile on her face handling our guests with aplomb. She was also probably wondering where in blazes I was. I pulled myself together and headed for the stairs. I would just have to postpone my midlife crisis, too.

I was startled to see how many people now occupied the downstairs. Most of them were unfamiliar to me. By one o'clock, the house was filled to bursting, and the noise level rose in direct correlation to the consumption of champagne. I oozed through the crowd in the hallway to take a break in my bedroom and change into something a bit less casual. I closed the door quietly behind me and went to find Jasmine. She looked calmly at me from her snug bed, which sat on the end of the couch, and I sat down beside her to give her a scritch.

"Sorry about the solitary confinement, old girl, but you wouldn't like it out there." Once again, her deafness was a blessing, sparing her undue stress from the crowd noises outside the door. I remembered that Jeff and Donna were due any minute and hurried to change from my sweater and slacks into a cream-colored suit. The cut of the jacket was ladylike, with a touch of tulle at the collar and wrists, and the short, fitted skirt that showed my legs to advantage always made Armando smile. I slipped my feet into matching high-heeled sandals and tidied away my things. Donna would need a sanctuary of her own, especially if she was still feeling queasy.

I could never understand the custom of combining the marriage ceremony, which is a pretty fraught undertaking all by itself, with a huge party. By the time the celebration gets started, the bride and groom always look glassy eyed, and one wonders if they can even begin to enjoy the event. Then, just when the party is getting good, they are whisked away from their friends to the airport for the honeymoon trip.

It's a good thing photographers commemorate the occasion, I thought. *If they didn't, the bride and groom probably wouldn't remember or even know about half of the day's events.* I paused with one hand on the doorknob. Among all the lists and menus, had there been any mention of a photographer?

I squeezed my way back down the hall to the living room and waved frantically at Joey, who stood next to a very pale Justine. She smiled at me gamely. I admired her pluck, but was she really well enough to be here?

"Joey!" I hissed, and he made his way through the crowd to my side. "We forgot about a photographer. We've got to have pictures. I need you to get to WalMart or CVS and buy a dozen of those disposable cameras with the built-in film. We'll just hand them out to people and hope for the best. Use my debit card. The code is your birthday."

"Got it," he said, "but I'll pay for them, Ma. I forgot to get Jeff and Donna a wedding present, so this can be it." Without even stopping to put on his jacket, he flew out the front door, almost colliding with a pleasant-faced woman on the porch. Her sober attire and briefcase identified her as the Justice of the Peace, here to officiate, but her whimsically spiked gray hair lightened the overall impression.

"Julie McKenna," she introduced herself, and I greeted her warmly. I had forgotten all about a J.P., too, and was glad that Michael, or more probably Sheila, had not.

"I'm Kate Lawrence, the groom's aunt, and the young man who nearly knocked you over is my son Joey, Jeff's cousin. Do come in."

Julie slipped out of her coat, and I attempted to find an empty hanger in the front hall closet. When I turned around, she and Henry were giggling together in the kitchen as wait staff milled around them.

"May I assume no introductions are needed here?"

"None at all," Julie assured me. "Henry and I have ushered dozens of couples through their wedding days. What's the menu today?" When I left the kitchen, Julie was ooohing and aaahing over a plate of hot hors d'oeuvres Henry pulled out of the oven.

By one-thirty, the pre-wedding party was in full swing. Armando had finally appeared, dressed in a navy blazer, unbuttoned, and dark gray slacks. As usual, he looked good enough to eat, Henry's *hors d'oeuvres* notwithstanding. Even the younger women in the crowd eyed him covetously, I thought. Henry leered openly, waggling his eyebrows at me Groucho Marx-style.

"Hands off, he's taken," I told him firmly, but I smiled while I said it.

Once again, I was filled with gratitude for my terrific,

grown-up children. Emma moved easily among the dozens of young people I didn't even know. Some seemed familiar to her, which surprised me. Apparently, she kept in better touch with her cousin than I had realized. When Joey reappeared with a shopping bag full of disposable cameras, he distributed them to Michael, Sheila, Emma, and an assortment of Jeff's and Donna's friends. When I begged off, pleading hostess duties, he handed the last one to Mary. She hooted with glee.

"Where's the happy couple? We need a few shots of the bride getting into her dress," she hollered to me across the room.

The steady hum of conversation around me waned and faltered. It seemed that all the guests craned their necks in my direction, waiting to hear my reply, but I realized I didn't have one. Julie, Henry and his staff all gazed at me, eyes bright with interest, while Emma and I locked eyes with one thought between us. *Yes, where are Jeff and Donna?*

A white-coated waiter appeared at my side. He spoke quietly, mindful of the sudden hush. "There's a phone call for you, Ms. Lawrence." He flicked his eyes right and left, then leaned in closer. "You'll probably want to take it in the kitchen."

"So it wasn't morning sickness or the pre-wedding jitters," I reported mournfully after hanging up the phone. "Donna has the full-blown, gut-wrenching flu, Jeff says, and it hit him, too, about an hour ago. They're a mess. The wedding's off."

Margo, Emma, Joey and Armando had followed me into the kitchen and stood in varying attitudes of dejection against the counters. An odd light came into Armando's eyes, almost as if he were enjoying this development, but I didn't have time to pursue it.

"Um, Sweetie?" Henry, ever unflappable, stayed focused on practical issues. "My heavenly luncheon is about ten minutes from ruin, and unless you give this crowd something substantial to eat very soon, you're going to have sixty sloppy drunks on your hands." He smiled kindly at me and raised his eyebrows.

"He's right, Sugar," Margo agreed. "That is one well-lubricated gatherin' out there, and there's no point lettin' Henry's wonderful food go to waste."

Henry bowed slightly from the waist in acknowledgment of the compliment. Joey and Emma nodded in agreement.

"We'll be telling this story at family functions for years," Emma predicted and came over to give me a hug.

"Face it, Ma," said Joey, waving to Justine, who hovered uncertainly in the doorway. "Come on in, Honey. It's not a wedding anymore, but it's still a really great party."

"I don't suppose you two would care to take advantage of the amenities and tie the knot?" I asked half-jokingly. To her credit, Justine took my teasing in stride.

"Maybe next time," she said lightly, and the way Joey looked at her confirmed my feeling that the next time wouldn't be long in coming.

I heaved a sigh that came up from my toes, which were beginning to hurt from standing around in high heels. I kicked off my sandals and held them in one hand.

"Okay, it's official. The wedding is off. Let the party begin. Henry, break out the appetizers. Sorry, Julie," I said as she wandered into the kitchen to investigate. She took the news philosophically.

"Happens more than you'd think. At least no one's crying this time. Mind if I hang around and have some lunch?" She winked at Armando rather mysteriously, I thought.

"Please," I said. "It's the least we can do."

Emma and Joey went to spread the word. I frankly didn't want to be present when Michael and Sheila got the news and slipped down the hall to my bedroom sanctuary. Armando was right behind me. We eased the door closed and flopped onto the sofa, where Jasmine lay napping in the afternoon sunshine. As usual, she was thrilled to see Armando and hustled over to climb into his lap.

"Why is it that you never greet me in this way?" he teased me. He stroked the old cat gently, and she closed her eyes in bliss.

"Oh, I don't know. I have my moments," I replied, and we both smiled a little, remembering some of them.

We sat quietly, listening to Jasmine's purr and the muted party sounds outside the door.

"You know," Armando broke the silence, "all of these people went to a great deal of trouble to attend a wedding this afternoon. It seems a shame to disappoint them."

He continued to pet Jasmine, but the strange light I had first noticed in his eyes in the kitchen had returned. My heart thumped in sudden understanding, and my own eyes widened. We sat for another minute, not daring to look at each other.

"We couldn't," I said finally.

"Actually, we could," he replied.

"We don't have a license."

"We can get it tomorrow. There's no waiting period in Wethersfield."

"And you know this because?"

"Because Julie just explained it to me. She will be happy to walk us through the paperwork tomorrow and to perform the ceremony this afternoon."

"You already discussed this with her?" I asked in amazement.

He raised one shoulder and let it fall. "It seemed a good time to ask some questions of someone who would know the answers."

"What about rings? We don't have any."

"Those also can be purchased tomorrow. In the meantime, we could borrow the rings of Donna and Jeff, which the best friend ..."

"Best man," I corrected automatically.

"... best man has in his pocket."

I looked at him.

"I know this because he was showing them to Emma," he answered my unspoken question.

"You don't think they'd mind?"

"I think they would be very glad to know that the rings they intended to be used at a wedding today were indeed used at a wedding today."

"Sort of a good luck road test," I joked.

"An omen of happiness to come for all four of us," Armando put it more gracefully. "So, *Cara*. Will you marry me?"

Fourteen

So it came to pass that two days after Christmas, surrounded by friends and family, two cats, my ex-husband, and a lot of complete strangers, Armando and I ate, drank—and were married. After all the complications of the preceding week in other areas, there was only one minor hitch in these proceedings, and we all agreed later that it was well worth it.

When Julie got to the point in the ceremony where she asked the assemblage if anyone present knew any reason why Armando and I should not be legally wed, I whispered in Armando's ear, "This is where I'd expect Strutter to make some smart-ass remark." Then I stared at him, stricken. "Strutter!" I blurted to Margo and Emma, who stood close by.

They both got it immediately, as did Armando. Julie was understandably bemused. "Just a minute, please," I begged her. "This is so important."

"No problem," she assured me and stood waiting calmly.

In one smooth movement, Emma fished her cell phone

out of her blazer pocket and handed it to Margo. She punched in Strutter's phone number and passed the phone to me.

"Putnam's House of Germs," Strutter answered dully. "Plenty for everyone, no waiting."

"Try to pay attention," I pleaded with her, "or you're going to miss the whole thing, and trust me, this is one wedding you don't want to miss."

"Kate? I'm sure your nephew and his fiancée are as cute as they can be, but I've never even met them."

"Not Jeff and Donna," I hissed. "Armando and I. The kids both got sick with the same thing you have, and we have all this food and champagne, and everyone's here. We've been talking about getting married for more than a year now, and today, it just feels right somehow." Armando nudged me, and I became aware of sixty pairs of ears hanging on my every word. "It's a long story, too long to go into at the moment," I concluded hastily. "The point is, we're standing in the living room getting married right now, but I just can't do it without you."

There was a moment of silence as Strutter tried to decide if I was playing a joke on her. Then, "Where are you exactly?"

"In front of the fireplace. Well, in front of Julie, who's the Justice of the Peace, but she's in front of the fireplace."

"Who's there besides Julie?"

I looked around, smiling. "Emma and Joey, Justine, Margo and John, Michael and Sheila and Sheila's mother Mitzi, our neighbor Mary ..."

"Hi, Strutter," each one called out in turn.

"Michael is there?" she gasped.

"Well, of course," I confirmed. "It's his nephew's wedding, or at least, it was supposed to be."

I heard Strutter sigh. "Only you could get married with your ex-husband standing in the room. Never mind. Go on."

I named all the names I knew for the faces in the crowd, ending with, "and of course, Henry Kozlowski and his staff."

"You mean Henri from the gala? That's amazing," Strutter murmured. "Okay, I'm up to speed. Give the phone to Margo, and let's do this."

I complied happily and took Armando's arm.

"Okay now?" Julie asked.

"Good to go," I assured her. Relieved laughter rippled through the room, and half a minute later, Armando and I each said, "I do," while Margo held the phone up in the air so Strutter could hear us. It wasn't the same as having her there in person, but it was way better than not having her there at all.

After five minutes of hugs and kisses, I insisted that luncheon be served. To Henry's great relief, his menu had held up beautifully despite the protracted delay, and the cheerful clink of silverware on china replaced much of the conversation as hungry guests dug in.

I hadn't seen him arrive, but Margo assured me that John had made it in time to see the ceremony. As soon as I decently could, I buttonholed him in the front hall to see how things had gone with James O'Halloran.

"Okay, I think. Margo put Mary in touch with an attorney who specializes in involuntary manslaughter cases, and from what I know of this case, it definitely qualifies. James might have to do a little time in a minimum security facility, but I really doubt it. He'll also get some help from a professional therapist who can help him deal with the consequences of his actions over the years."

"What about Mary? How's she doing?"

He chuckled. "She's a real bulldog, that one. It sounds like a funny thing to say, under the present circumstances, but O'Halloran is one lucky guy."

"So are you, you know. Margo might kill you herself one of these days, but she will also move heaven and earth to keep anyone else from hurting you."

He grinned at me. "As you would for Armando and as Strutter would for her husband. It's called love, Lady."

Late in the afternoon, most of the young people drifted out the front door and back to their lives, after assuring Armando and me that the unexpected substitution of bride and groom had been, as one of them put it, "a real hoot." As Henry/Henri refilled my champagne glass, I looked around at the eclectic group of family and friends who still mingled contentedly in the living room. Armando had put a match to the logs in the fireplace, and Emma and Margo had set out every candle they could find in the house.

Added to the glow of the Christmas tree, the effect was warm and mellow.

Across the way stood my brand new husband, holding a glass of champagne in one hand and a plate of wedding cake in the other. Emma and Joey, friends again, kidded each other good naturedly over who would be next to take vows. Full of shrimp, Jasmine dozed by the fire, blessed yet again by the deafness that allowed her to enjoy this moment without alarm, since Gracie still preferred the safety of Armando's bedroom.

In a corner of the dining room, my ex-husband and his new wife chatted easily with the remaining guests, all of whom seemed perfectly at ease with the surprising turn of events. Even Sheila's ditzy mother had found the perfect companion in our crazy neighbor Mary. The two cackled gleefully as they swapped stories on the couch near the fireplace.

Armando caught my eye and raised his glass. I blew him a kiss in return. *Today's extended family,* I thought. *Welcome to suburban America in the new millennium.* It might not work for everyone, but against all odds, it seemed to work for us. Throughout this bizarre holiday week, we had been with the people we cared about and who cared about us in return.

Images from the past few days chased each other through my mind. Sister Marguerite and the good folks at the UCC struggling to tend to those in need ... Margo and Strutter dropping everything to help out at the gala ... Armando appearing on Christmas eve with a stray cat under his coat ... the swelling organ music in the cathedral ... dear John guiding us through the O'Halloran situation ... the coyotes feasting on our ruined turkey ... Strutter's mom flying straight to her daughter's side in her time of need ... James O'Halloran, willing to vanish into exile to spare his wife one more moment's pain ... Mary O'Halloran standing on tiptoe to cuss out her husband and then hug him ... the burly truck driver who stopped traffic to allow a goose to cross the road ... Emma and Joey squabbling, then making up ... and now this surprising gift of a new beginning with a man I adored.

John Harkness had been absolutely right, I decided as I gazed at the dilapidated angel atop our tree. She had seen us all through half a century of good years and bad, and still she perched on the topmost twig, a little the worse for wear but still hopeful. Christmas wasn't always wrapped in holiday carols and tinsel. It didn't have to be roast goose and chestnuts on an open fire, however that worked anyway. It was about love in its many varieties, all of them wonderful and life affirming, and that spelled Christmas to me.

Epilog
Saturday, March 20th

No matter how long you live in New England, spring always comes as a delightful surprise. January seems to last forever, but suddenly it's mid-February, and you're not driving home from work in the dark anymore. March comes howling in, usually accompanied by a big, wet snowstorm. Then one morning, there's a softness in the breeze, and you notice that the robins are back. You can smell damp earth, and yes, the crocuses are pushing up on the sheltered side of the front porch. You find yourself smiling at strangers for no particular reason. *Made it through another one,* we say as we turn our faces toward the sun.

In precisely that frame of mind, Margo, Strutter and I sprawled luxuriously on the benches grouped to the side of the Keeney Memorial Cultural Center on Old Main Street. We all sipped at cups of hot coffee Margo had picked up at the diner for us. Baby Olivia staggered along next to her mother's bench, holding on for dear life and drunk with the power of being vertical. Rhett Butler, Margo's adoring chocolate Lab, looked on with appropriate avuncular attentiveness.

"For once, the first day of spring actually feels like it,"

Margo observed. Her eyes were closed as she basked in the promising warmth.

"Mmmm," Strutter agreed, "but I have more reasons than that to be happy this spring."

Margo opened her eyes, and I raised a questioning eyebrow.

"For one thing, nobody in my house currently has the flu, and for another, I'm not nine and a half months pregnant like I was at this time last year."

We agreed that those were excellent reasons for celebration.

"Besides, it's Margo's turn to welcome a new addition to the family," she added.

My jaw dropped, but Margo remained composed. "Yup," she agreed cheerfully. "Rhett here is goin' to be a daddy, so to speak." The dog panted happily at the sound of his adored mistress's voice. "I couldn't bring myself to go with John to the rescue center. I'd want to bring every one of those darlin' puppies home. So John picked out our baby girl. At least, that's what he says, but it's my personal feelin' she picked him out. She's a mixed breed with enough big dog in her gene pool to make her a good size when she's fully grown."

"I hope they turn out to be better friends than Jasmine and Gracie," I said, thinking of recent hostilities between my two felines. We had wanted to give Jasmine a new interest in life, but so far, her main interest in Gracie seemed to be hissing and spitting at the newcomer. "Well, at least Jasmine isn't sleeping twenty-four hours a day, and her appetite has certainly improved."

Olivia lurched her way to the end of the bench nearest to me and held out one hand. Bits of leaves and twigs were clutched in her pudgy fingers.

"Ngah?" she inquired, staring at me intently.

"Very nice," I agreed. "Go show them to Auntie Margo." I helped her negotiate the turn, and she tottered laboriously in Margo's direction as Strutter chuckled.

I contemplated Old Main Street over the rim of my paper cup. The effects of the past year's disastrous economy were all too evident. Comstock Ferre, the gardening center that had anchored the little business district for as many years as I could remember, had closed its doors, as had Mainly Tea, our beloved tea shop. A Space to Let sign flapped forlornly in front of the Law Barn, the former home of MACK Realty.

Still, signs of hope were popping up all over town. A new pasta shop had opened on the Silas Deane Highway and seemed to be doing very well. The new owners of the Henstock sisters' crumbling Victorian on the Broad Street Green had turned it into a breathtaking bed-and-breakfast that was enjoying good word of mouth. Abby Dalton, who owned the Village Diner, had taken on a new waitress to accommodate an uptick in business, and even now, painters were busy spiffing up the exterior of the drugstore down the block from us.

Of even more interest to the three of us, the real estate market, which had all but dried up in the past year, was finally showing signs of returning life.

"Wonder who has that listin'?" Margo peered at a For Sale sign in front of a genteel bungalow on Church Street across the way from us. "I can't quite see it from here."

"Bet you could see it if you wore your glasses for once in your life," Strutter told her. She wriggled around to have a look. "Prudential. Huh." Her tone said it all. *Wish we had the listing,* was our common thought and was, in fact, the reason for our gathering this morning.

"So, do you think it's time to reopen MACK Realty?" I asked the question for all of us.

"Since we still represent Vista Views, we never really closed, technically speaking," Strutter reminded me.

"You know what I mean." I nodded in the direction of the Law Barn.

"It's too soon to risk the expense of rentin' a big place like that, especially since Emma and Isabel have set up shop in that cute little place in Glastonbury," Margo stated. "I think the two of you should look for a place like that. You know, small and manageable."

Strutter and I exchanged a look. "The two of us?" I asked carefully.

Margo caught my tone and reached over to pat my knee. "Don't go getting' your knickers in a twist, Sugar. I'm not abandonin' ship. I'll still do Vista Views and take an occasional house listin', but more than that would interfere with my campaign."

Now she really had our attention. "Campaign?" we chorused, thunderstruck.

Margo smiled gently at us and smoothed her already

perfect hair. "John and I have been talkin' about it for a while now. At first, I thought it was a crazy idea, but John has convinced me that I'd make an absolutely wonderful addition to the Town Council."

It took several seconds for Strutter to locate her voice. "I'm sure you would. You know I believe you can do anything you put your mind to, but the Town Council? That would require, um, getting elected."

Margo nodded. "Thus, the campaign."

"But you're a blonde bombshell from Atlanta, Georgia," I pointed out unnecessarily. "New Englanders elect candidates with strong ties to New England."

"Oh, don't you worry about that, Sugar. My husband's family tree has roots all the way back to the Mayflower," she smiled. "It also doesn't hurt a bit that he's a big, good lookin' homicide detective who just solved a major crime." She winked at me. "Of course, he had a little help from a friend."

I did my best to look modest, probably unsuccessfully.

"Speaking of major crime, how did things turn out with the O'Hallorans?" Strutter wanted to know.

"James was clearly distraught," Margo reported, "and Joseph's death was ruled accidental. It was the attempted cover up and the running away part that threw a monkey wrench into the proceedings, and for that, James got a one-year sentence for obstruction of justice, suspended. He's receiving court-appointed therapy, which is the best part."

"Was he allowed to return to work?" Strutter asked. I knew the answer to that one.

"He was, I'm happy to say. As Sister Marguerite put it, they would be poor excuses for Christians if they didn't stand by one of their own, and James has devoted his professional life to the UCC. He can't actually function as the Chief Financial Officer and sign documents and financial reports and so on. His former assistant has been promoted to that role, but there's plenty of work for James to do. Mary says he's more than willing to accept a diminished role. In fact, he seems to be relieved at having less responsibility. I think he's going to be fine."

"What about Mary's feelin's in all of this?" asked Margo.

I turned the question back to her. "If this had happened to John, what would your feelings be?"

She smiled slowly. "Gotcha. What about the little boy?"

"Patrick? That's probably the best part of all. Now that the secret of Patrick is out in the open, James is free to be a part of his life, and Mary couldn't be happier about it. They're going out to California together in a couple of weeks to visit Patrick. If things work out as they all hope, Mary may finally have a little boy to mother from time to time in the coming years."

Olivia let go of the bench and held up her arms to her mother, wavering precariously. Strutter scooped her into her lap, where the little girl snuggled contentedly and stuck her thumb into her mouth.

"Time to get this one home for a nap," she announced. Reluctantly, we all got to our feet. I collected the cups for the trash basket, and we strolled to our cars, which were parked at the curb. "By the way, after you and Armando stole their thunder, whatever happened with Jeff and Donna?"

"Got over the flu and eloped to Mexico," I said with satisfaction. "Had a fabulous time at one of those all-inclusive couples places."

"As long as we're tyin' up loose ends, how's Emma doin' after the bad break-up?" Margo asked. Again, I was glad to give my friends good news.

"It took her about ten minutes to get over the big jerk and maybe another ten to decide to go to a New Year's party thrown by an old friend from high school. A fellow in her class that she had always liked but never quite connected with back then also showed up at the party, and the rest, as they say, is history. I don't think they've been apart since."

"Promisin'," Margo agreed.

Strutter nodded as she straightened up from fastening Olivia securely into her car seat. "I guess it wasn't such a terrible Christmas after all," was her comment.

Margo and I laughed raucously, and Strutter looked sheepish, then giggled. "Okay, it was terrible," she admitted, "but you have to admit that things have been uphill from there."

"Okay, Pollyanna," I chided her affectionately, "you get the last word."

About Judith K. Ivie

A lifelong Connecticut resident, Judith Ivie has worked in public relations, advertising, sales promotion, and the international tradeshow industry. She has also served as administrative assistant to several top executives.

Along the way, Judi also produced three nonfiction books, as well as numerous articles and essays. Her nonfiction focus is on work issues such as two-career marriages, workaholism, and midlife career changes. Second editions of *Calling It Quits: Turning Career Setbacks to Success* and *Working It Out: The Domestic Double Standard* are available from Whiskey Creek Press in trade paperback and downloadable electronic formats.

A few years back, Judi broadened her repertoire to include fiction, and the Kate Lawrence mystery series was launched.

Whatever the genre, she strives to provide lively, entertaining reading that takes her readers away from their work and worries for a few hours, stimulates thought on a variety of contemporary issues-and gives them a laugh along the way.

Please visit **www.JudithIvie.com** to learn more about all of her books, or order her other titles. Judi loves to hear from readers at Ivie4@hotmail.com.

9 780982 795255